THE SPIN

A DAY IN MY SHOES

MALIKA CARTER

THE SPIN

The Spin Copyright © 2025 by Malika Carter. No part of this publication may be reproduced, distributed, or transmitted in any form or by any means, including photocopying, Recording, or other electronic or mechanical methods, without the prior written permission of the publisher, except in the case of brief quotations embodied in critical reviews and certain other noncommercial uses permitted by copyright law. All rights reserved.

I have tried to recreate events, locales and conversations from my memories of them. In order to maintain their anonymity in some instances, I have changed the names of individuals and places. I may have changed some identifying characteristics and details such as physical properties, occupations and places of residence.

For permission requests, email the publisher:
info@JacinthMediaProductions.com

All Scripture quotes are taken from the Holy Bible, King James Version, Cambridge, 1769; and The ESV® Bible
(The Holy Bible, English Standard Version®).
ESV® Text Edition: 2016. Copyright © 2001 by Crossway,
A publishing ministry of Good News Publishers.

Paperback-ISBN: 978-1-960594-22-8
Hardback-ISBN: 978-1-960594-21-1
Ebook-ISBN: 978-1-960594-23-5
This book was printed in the United States
First Printing
10 9 8 7 6 5 4 3 2 1
Book cover design by Jacinth Media Productions

TABLE OF CONTENTS

PROLOGUE

Winter in the pen was known to be below zero, but this winter in particular was beyond brutal. Linette found herself pregnant and trapped in a hellhole prison, feeling the painful weight of the world on her shoulders. This wasn't just any pain. It was the kind that rips through your body—unbearable. And the guards? They didn't give a damn.

The contractions ripped through her like a thunderstorm, but those heartless guards wouldn't even let her see the damn nurse. The chaos swallowed Linette, and she was knocked out cold on the hard concrete. Would you believe they threw her in the hole just because she defended herself against the other inmates?

One day all hell broke loose in that godforsaken place. The damn correctional officers, heartless as they come, didn't give two craps about her condition. They didn't even care that she was carrying life inside her...No! They put the whole damn prison on lockdown.

Eight months pregnant, Linette was in pain

from a fall she previously had. She begged the guards to be transferred to the hospital for medical treatment, but they refused and told her she had to wait until the next day. Scared for her baby's life, Linette started to panic, and all she could do was cry and pray.

On March 2, at 11:00 p.m., Linette started having back-to-back contractions until she became 8 centimeters dilated. Linette yelled out in severe pain as she desperately sought help.

"I think I'm in labor!" She screamed out with her voice carrying the weight of her pain, but the guard on shift didn't pay her any mind. He just kept on working, like her suffering meant nothing to him. A few minutes later, Linette screamed out.

"Help!" As she felt a sharp pop in her stomach. Suddenly her water broke — a flood of fluid gushed between her legs with the imminent arrival of her baby.

But those heartless guards didn't care. Although her water broke and she was leaking fluid, the guard told her she had to sit in her cell for a couple more hours until the shift changed over. Her heart shattered as she cried, tears mingling with desperation. *How can they be so damn heartless?*

"Let me out, please. If anything happens to my baby, I am suing everyone up in here!" She yelled out from behind her cell's door.

Finally, the ambulance showed up. Linette was rushed to the hospital with her feet and hands shackled to the gurney.

Labor pain and giving birth was already a hard experience; now she had to give birth in shackles. Linette fought through all the pain and agony of having to endure being in labor for 10 hours.

And then the moment arrived. On March 3 at 5:30 p.m., her precious baby girl came into this world, screaming her first breath. Linette named her Kachelle, a symbol of hope amidst the dark, twisted reality. But even in that moment of triumph, joy was stripped away from her. Kwame, Linette's baby's father, was home worried sick about her, as he anticipated a phone call with updates on Linette and his baby. Unfortunately, he was not allowed to come to the hospital to see Linette give birth due to prison regulations and restrictions.

Initially, he was unaware of Linette being in labor because he didn't receive any phone calls. Linette was not allowed to make phone calls because it was after the allowed calling hours.

As soon as she gave birth, her baby girl was taken from her arms with no time to bond. Linette was hysterical.

"Please don't take my baby. I want to hold her for a little while longer, please!" Linette cried out.

As the jail guards were watching and waiting to take her back to jail, the nurse turned and looked at Linette.

"I'm sorry, but I have to take the baby now." Linette was completely heartbroken and in disbelief, wondering how this could even be lawful and legal. A baby needs its mom's nurturing.

Kwame finally got the call from the warden, instructing him on when and where he should be able to pick up his baby girl. After giving birth and having a day's rest at the hospital, Linette was transferred back to prison where she would finish the rest of her sentence.

Things were still rough for Linette, as she began experiencing deep depression from missing her baby girl. Not only was she without her baby, but she was in deep pain, as her oversized breasts were sore and tender. Not only was she dealing with the pain in her breasts, but she was also waking up in the middle of the night with so much breast pain that milk leaked out of her like a water hose. She was very sad and depressed about the whole situation and couldn't believe how people could be so heartless.

Linette was stuck in her cell in deep thought, with tears running down her face as she tried to make sense of her life. She questioned whether life was still worth living anymore.

CHAPTER 1
LOVE AT FIRST SIGHT

Ever heard of the saying *love at first sight?* Well, this was Linette and Kwame's reality — their teenage love affair. They both met at a local fair and couldn't take their eyes off each other. When Linette first laid eyes on Kwame, she stopped right in her tracks. Although they were only 16 years old, they knew they had something special.

Linette always yearned for a father's love. She was raised by a single mom, named Netta, and they were dirt poor. She didn't have a father figure, and all the men her mom brought into their lives were toxic. Linette witnessed her mom get abused and cheated on constantly.

She grew resentful of men and her mom; she couldn't understand why her mom would bring these low-life men around knowing they were toxic. She lost all respect for her mom and hated the father she never got to know. All she knew about her father was of him being a well-known pimp who sold drugs for a living and was in and out of jail. Linette was left with no other option but to seek love and nurturing in the streets. Just like her father, all she knew was the streets for survival. The apple didn't fall too far from the tree.

The street was the home that made sure she was fed, clothed, and able to purchase her first car at 16, but nothing in life is free. Little did Linette know there was a price to pay for the weekly allowance she was getting from the local drug dealer.

She never received an allowance from her mother. Whenever she asked, her mother would curse her out and chase her out of the house. Linette started selling drugs at the age of 15, right around the time she joined the basketball team. She wanted her mom to buy her a pair of basketball sneakers, but her mom cursed her out and told her she didn't have any *'fucking money for sneakers*!'

In Linette's heart, she wanted to finish school and become successful. She never thought that selling drugs would be her only way of life, but her need for money led her to run into a well-known drug supplier named Monkey. Monkey started fronting Linette work, and he would usually give her a time frame to pay him back his money. Things started slowly for Linette because she had to learn the game and how it was played. After she got the swing of everything, her money started to flow, and she was able to purchase her first car by age 16. She bought a two-door Toyota Celica GT. She was super excited to finally have wheels to get around to push her work and to show off her independence. Although she didn't know anything about car ownership and how to register her vehicle, she felt unstoppable and proud.

Linette's mom was very angry when she found out Linette had purchased a car without her permission. She began to question her about her whereabouts and how she was getting money. She even questioned her non-stop about selling drugs and where did she get the car from? Linette refused to answer her. She had no respect for her mom.

"Don't worry about what I'm doing to get my money because every time I ask you for some money, you always tell me, NO! So, I have to get it the best way I know how."

"Get the fuck out my house!" Netta then yelled. Linette left her mom's house and went to stay with her grandma, Bea, who loved her dearly. Linette finally felt comfortable here than at home because she had a better relationship with her grandmother.

Linette continued going to school and was finally able to purchase the basketball sneakers she always wanted. Now that she had them, she finally can play on the school basketball team.

However, nothing else changed because she continued selling drugs after school because she had her debts to pay. Money started flowing for Linette, and she was at the top of her game. Most local round-the-way niggas couldn't even step to Linette. She not only bossed up but leveled up.

Linette finally earned the respect she worked so hard for, which started to get to her head. She is one of the youngest *bitches* getting money on her block. Not to mention, she was delivering top-notch quality products. That kept her clients loyal to her and happy.

One day on a nice July evening, Linette and her girls decided to go to the local fair that comes to town every summer. Now that Linette's money was right, and she had her own car to drive, she could come and go as she pleased. Especially since her Grandma Bea was now getting older and couldn't get around much, which gave Linette all the freedom in the world.

At the fair, Linette and her girls played games, got on rides, and enjoyed funnel cakes and cotton candy. She then ran into her cousin Jaden and his boy Kwame who was fairly new in town. Linette and Jaden were both shocked to see each other after many years. They hugged and started talking like they never skipped a beat... just like old times.

"Who's your friend?" Linette asked right away.

"Oh, this is my boy Kwame who just moved next door to me," Jaden replied with a smile.

Both Kwame and Linette introduced themselves to one another, locking eyes instantly. It was obvious they were really feeling each other.

Boldly, Linette walked up to Kwame wasting no time shooting out questions.

"Do you have a girl?"

Shyly, Kwame shook his head *no*.

Linette whispered softly into his ear. "Well, you do now."

They both started laughing as Kwame blushed and smiled from ear to ear. They continued to enjoy the night as they rode the Ferris wheel. Linette couldn't remember the last time she laughed this hard and felt this happy. All she knew was that it felt damn good.

As Linette and her girls were leaving the fair, Kwame kept his gaze on Linette as if he was hypnotized watching as she began driving away in her new car. This turned him on.

CHAPTER 2
YOUNG LOVE

Now, let's talk about Kwame, a Leo who was born on August 5th, 1975, and raised in a household with four sisters and no brothers. He was the third child and the only boy.

Life for Kwame was not always easy. He grew up in an abusive household, and his family became homeless when their house caught on fire due to his stepdad burning his mother's clothes while they were all still home. To save her son, who was then nine years old, Kwame's mom, Cookie, sent him to live with his paternal grandmother, Mable, who was from Jamaica. Kwame's grandma loved him so much but was still stern like the typical Caribbean elder.

Being raised in the church, Kwame sang lead in the youth choir and served on the usher board. He served faithfully in the church with his grandma Mable until he turned 15 years old and had to move back with his mom. Kwame's mother was newly divorced and wanted a new beginning for her and her family, so she decided to pack and relocate to a new town in Connecticut, which was where Kwame and Linette first met each other at the fair. Kwame's mother also loved the Lord and was now back to serving faithfully in her local church. Kwame was excited to be back in church and was able to join the choir. Kwame finally started to feel at home as he gained new friends and got familiar with the neighborhood.

About a week later, after seeing Kwame at the fair, Linette couldn't get over how fine and chocolatey Kwame was. She remembered her cousin Jaden stated that Kwame was his next-door neighbor who had just moved to town, so Linette drove over to her cousin's house and started beeping the horn very loudly, yelling for Jaden to come outside. As soon as Jaden heard the car horn and came running outside disheveled and shouting.

"Cuz, what the fuck is your problem beeping that horn outside like that? Are you crazy!?"

"Yes, I am! I'm trying to get your neighbor to come outside with his fine ass." Jaden started laughing.

"Cousin, you crazy! You betta not fuck this nigga head up. He's a good dude, he goes to school, and he's not in these streets. We not out here selling drugs. We still on the bus line."

"Yo, cuz, watch your mouth, and mind your business. Like I said, call yo boy outside."

"I don't think he's home, but I'll tell him you looking for him when I talk to him."

"Whatever," Linette kissed her teeth then pulled off.

Now that Linette had gotten more into the drug game, she started going out hustling on her block before it was time to go to school.

One morning, Linette woke up early and headed out to the block. Before leaving the house, her Grandma Bea noticed her getting up earlier than usual. She began interrogating her.

"Where are you going so early? It's not time for your school yet."

"Don't worry, Grandma, I'm alright. I gotta go handle some business," Linette stated. Grandma Bea then yelled out to her.

"I'm praying for you girl! You better get your life together. I love you, but something isn't right."

Linette rushed out of the house and refused to listen to what her grandmother said. While out on the block, she attempted to make her first sale, but the cops ran up on her and found drugs in her pocket. Linette tried to run but didn't get far.

The cop caught up to her and restrained her until a female officer arrived to search Linette. She then read Linette her Miranda rights.

Now she was being held downtown on a drug charge. Linette was only allowed one phone call, which she used to call her mother, Netta.

Linette's mother answered the phone. Linette quickly began explaining to her that she was in jail. Netta paused. Then a rude awakening followed.

"Don't call me no more. YOU left my house after I told YOU not to be in the streets. YOU didn't want to listen. And you better NOT use my motherfuckin' address, either Goodbye!" Netta quickly hung up the phone after saying her two cents or three cents for that matter.

Linette was stuck in jail for the night and had to wait to go to court in the morning. Her car was towed by the police, so she would have to pay to get her car from the impound, which had no registration or insurance. She felt stuck and had no idea how she would get her car back.

The next morning, Linette went to see the judge, and she was granted a PTA (promise to appear) since it was her first time ever being in trouble but will not be her last. Linette was given a court date to appear for arraignment.

Now that Linette was free and back on the streets, she started the drug game fresh. The cops took all the drugs she had on her and all the money she had stashed in her car. Linette had to go meet up with Monkey, who was not happy at all with what happened to the work and money she had for him. Not only did she get arrested and have the car towed by the police, but she still owed him money.

Linette talked with Monkey and convinced him to get her car out of the pound and to front her more work, promising that she would quit school and be on the block day in and day out until he was paid back every dime that she owed him. He finally agreed to release her.

Linette finally got her car back and got some money in her pocket, yet she was still thinking about Kwame even after all the drama. She drove over to her cousin's house in hopes of seeing his friend Kwame. Just her luck, she spotted him helping his mother bring in groceries. Kwame noticed her car and then signaled with his forefinger for her to wait a minute for him. Kwame hurried and finished helping his mom as he ran back outside to speak with Linette. Quickly, she exited the car and walked towards him.

"I came by here looking for you a couple of weeks ago. Did my cousin tell you?"

"Yea, he told me you were out here going crazy for me." Kwame chuckled. They then burst out in laughter.

The two sat on his porch and started to talk as they got to know each other. It was starting to get dark, and Kwame's mom, Cookie, shouted for him to come inside the house to prep for school tomorrow. Linette quickly asked Kwame what school he went to so she could pick him up after school.

The two of them started to become best friends right away. They began a friendly relationship. Kwame's mom was very strict with him, and she did not allow him to hang out in the streets or be outside after dark. The fact that he and his family were new in town made her even more cautious.

This forced Linette and Kwame to talk even

more on the phone since his time outside was limited. Linette enjoyed picking Kwame up every day from school. Kwame's mother started to question Linette's age and how she was able to buy a car at such a young age. Kwame reassured his mom that Linette was a very nice girl and that they were just friends. To see him even longer, Linette started braiding his hair after picking him up from school. They both would fall asleep with each other while speaking on the phone. They had a teenage love but without any sex.

Once again Linette stopped going to school and became a full-time drug dealer on the streets. However, she got busted again, and this time she was looking at way more charges with longer time in jail. Linette tried to send a collect call to Netta, but she refused all her calls. Linette went to court, and the judge raised her bail bond even higher. Linette had no one who would come to her rescue, and she had to be in jail for two years.

On the day of her arrest, Kwame was waiting for her to pick him up from school as usual, but Linette never showed up. Kwame had to catch the school bus home. He was so sad on the bus ride home. All kinds of thoughts were going through his mind of what possibly happened to Linette because it wasn't like her to not be there after school. He rushed home to see if Linette had called his house phone, but there were no missed calls. Kwame later found out Linette was sentenced to two years in jail. They both lost touch with each other because he never heard from her and didn't know where she was sentenced.

CHAPTER 3
THE RECONNECTION

After two years had passed, Linette got out of jail, and all she could think about was finding Kwame. Since his mother was a single mom, she struggled to keep their house phone on, so Linette had no way to communicate with Kwame. She was hoping he didn't have a girlfriend while she was locked up. After being released, Linette went back to the old block before looking for Kwame. The niggas on the block were happy to see that she was out of jail and back home. Linette got right back to work like she never left. She stayed on block day in and day out until her pockets were back up again.

After she re-upped (restocking of drugs), she went and bought a new car, a Nissan wagon. Things were going well for Linette. Now she was on the hunt to find Kwame like old times. She picked the perfect time and drove to Kwame's bus stop, hoping to run up on him. No sooner than she reached the bus stop, Linette's heart dropped! She saw Kwame and another female walking home together caught up in a deep conversation. But that didn't stop her from driving close to them. Slowly, Linette rolled down her window.

"Oh, is that bitch braiding your hair now!?"

Kwame looked back recognizing a familiar voice coming from the car.

"Linette? What the hell are you talking about?"

Without a reply, Linette pulled off. Kwame was vexed and confused. He rushed home and tried to call her grandmother's number, but she was not there. He left numerous messages for her to call him back ASAP.

Before the night ended, Linette went by Kwame's house. She beeped the car horn for him to come outside. She apologized to him for her actions earlier, explaining that she missed him. She continued by expressing how sorry she was for being away from him for so long, pushing him into a relationship with someone else. Kwame explained to Linette that the girl she saw him with was just a friend and it was nothing serious going on with them.

Linette stayed out all night and got one of her crackheads to rent her a hotel room. Both Linette and Kwame spent the night and had sex for the very first time. They were stuck on cloud 9, and both thought they were in deep love. Things started to get more serious as Kwame and Linette set a dinner date so she could meet his mother and relatives. Linette started attending church with Kwame and his family. Kwame's family didn't really approve of Linette because of her lifestyle. Kwame's mom saw that her son was happy, but she also saw his behavior digressing as he continued staying out late at night with Linette then soon started missing school.

To make matters worse, Linette got busted again for drugs but was able to make bond. Kwame talked to her about not being in the streets and going back to school to finish her diploma. She listened to him and started night school because she would still be able to sell drugs during the daytime. Linette still didn't have a good relationship with her mom. Nevertheless, she brought Kwame to visit her family for Thanksgiving.

Linette's family was not too welcoming towards him. Her Grandma Bea was the only one who made him feel welcomed. Linette's mother, Netta, was there; however, the two didn't speak at all. Kwame really felt out of place, but that didn't stop his love for Linette. He still wanted to be with her.

Kwame left a good impression on Linette's Grandma Bea. She saw good potential in him and told him he was welcome to her home any time and gave him her house number.

CHAPTER 4
CROSSFIRE

One day while standing outside on her block, heavy gunfire erupted. Linette got caught in the crossfire. She was shot in the leg causing blood to squirt out everywhere. She was then rushed to her local hospital's emergency room where she underwent emergency surgery.

Netta received a call about her daughter and was worried her daughter might die. She only heard Linette had been shot. She didn't know the severity of her condition. Linette was in surgery for four hours as the doctors carefully removed the bullet. The surgeon was able to save the bones in Linette's ankle, but the damage was so severe, it left her with pins, screws, and rods in her ankle and leg.

Linette woke up from surgery to see her mother standing over her. She was elated to see her mom by her side because truth be told, she wanted to have a better relationship with her.

Meanwhile, Kwame had no idea what was going on because he had not heard from Linette in a week. Kwame reached out to Linette's cousin, Jaden, to see if he had heard from Linette. Jaden stated he was going to make some phone calls. Jaden had learned that Linette had been in the hospital from gunshot wounds. Jaden notified Kwame right away and told him what hospital she was at. Kwame walked to the hospital. When he got there, he saw Netta and immediately rushed over to greet her.

Linette's mom became very disrespectful towards Kwame. Kwame was lost for words and in shock at Netta's behavior. Kwame's heart was crushed by Netta, as he left with the hope Linette would contact him after she was released from the hospital.

After having two emergency surgeries, Linette was finally released from the hospital but was unable to walk or wear long pants. Linette was left in her mother's care and was now homebound.

She slept in a hospital bed at her mother's house for three years. She never heard from Kwame during any of that time. Soon, Linette began to reach out to him with hopes of reconnecting. They had not spoken to each other in months, due to her being in the hospital. Unbeknownst to Linette, her mom had turned him away.

Eventually, Linette made contact with Kwame. They were excited to hear each other's voice. As they reconnected, Kwame started skipping school his senior year just so he could take care of Linette when her mom was at work, especially since he wasn't allowed in her house while she was not there.

Kwame and Linette began having a sexual relationship thus falling deeper in love with one another. He helped nurse her back to health by bringing her food every day and keeping her company. He made sure her health was progressing, as she grew stronger each day.

Linette's lawyer notified the court that she had been shot and was unable to attend court for her pending cases. After two years of being homebound, Linette was starting to learn how to walk again, with Kwame right by her side the entire time.

Linette later found out she was pregnant and immediately called Kwame to tell him. He was ecstatic as he joyfully laughed.

"Who's the daddy?" He teased knowing the

answer.

"Stop playing." They promised each other to be the best parents they could be for their baby but were scared as hell to tell their families. Then to make matters worse, Linette became distraught when she learned she would be facing more charges and a lengthy jail sentence once she was able to walk again.

She went to her first medical appointment and found out her due date would be March 1, which was Cookie's birthday with Netta's birthday following on March 16. Cookie and Netta argued about not sharing their birthday month.

Surprisingly, Linette and Kwame were excited about the pregnancy. The hardest part although was going to be letting her mother know about the pregnancy. Netta has never been supportive of Linette which is the main reason for delaying the news.

Linette was now pregnant and walking around. She felt the need to get back to the streets more than ever before because she refused to have her baby struggle. She and Kwame had talked about being together as a family and not raising kids as single parents. Kwame dropped out of his last year in school and started looking for a day job and night school instead. Linette and Kwame went back and forth debating on names for the baby.

Finally, they both told Netta and Cookie about the pregnancy. Neither were happy about becoming grandparents.

CHAPTER 5
A MOTHER'S STRUGGLE IN JAIL

Linette, now six months pregnant, found herself back on the streets, facing trouble once again. This time, her pregnancy didn't save her from being arrested. All her past cases came up, and she was sentenced to eight years in jail (with four years suspended), despite being pregnant. Life took a sharp turn for Linette. Kwame had to visit her in jail, and things got complicated. On the brighter side, Netta and Kwame started getting along, and Netta even gave Kwame rides to visit Linette. Everything seemed fine, but things started to change.

Life in jail got harder by the day for Linette, especially being pregnant. The guards weren't kind, and she faced tough times. Her feet became swollen, and the sneakers they provided didn't fit. She had to cut them to make them fit.

While in jail this time, a fight broke out, and Linette got caught in it, even though she was pregnant. The guards didn't seem to care about her condition and put everyone on lockdown.

Life got even tougher for Linette. She was hungry, but they couldn't give her much food because of her pain. She was not getting the proper medical care she needed while being pregnant. Being in jail was really rough, and Linette worried about giving birth there. She knew she might have to give her baby to Kwame or Netta while she continued her sentence. She found out she was having a baby girl and shared the news with Kwame during a visit. They started thinking about names.

Kwame stepped up. He got a job and supported Linette by visiting her and sending letters. He also got his own place to take care of their baby when she was born. Netta helped him prepare for the baby. Kwame and Linette picked a name for the baby together, but in the meantime, Linette's experience in jail got worse. She took a GED course but faced difficulties. Her feet were still swollen, and a fight landed her in more trouble. She was even pushed down during the fight. The guards didn't care that she was pregnant and kept everyone on lockdown.

In jail, Linette's health started to get worse. She was in pain, her feet hurt, and she was leaking milk. The guards didn't help, and she was feeling sad and depressed. As the due date approached, Linette's life became a rollercoaster of emotions. Eight months pregnant, Linette was in pain from the fall she previously had. She begged the guards to be transferred to the hospital for medical treatment, but they refused her treatment and told her she must wait until the next day. Scared for her baby's life, Linette started to panic, and all she could do was cry and pray.

On March 2, at 11:00 p.m., Linette started having back-to-back contractions. By now, she was 8 centimeters dilated. Linette yelled out in severe pain as she desperately sought help.

"I think I'm in labor!"

The officer on the shift did not pay her any mind as he continued working. A few minutes later Linette screamed.

"Help!" Her water had just broken. Even with fluid leaking everywhere, the guard told her she had to sit in her cell for a couple more hours until the shift changed over. Linette was enraged. She began crying and thinking to herself, *how can these people be so heartless?*

"Let me out, please! If anything happens to my

baby, I am suing everyone up in here," she bawled out from behind her cell's door.

Finally, they showed up to take her to the hospital. Linette was rushed to the hospital in an ambulance with both feet and hands shackled to the gurney in labor. Giving birth was already a hard experience and now she had to give birth in shackles.

Linette fought through all the pain and agony of having to endure being in labor for 10 hours. She gave birth to a precious baby girl.

On March 3, at 5:30 p.m., Linette gave birth to a beautiful baby girl named Kachelle. Linette's baby's father, Kwame, was home pacing his living room floor panicking as he anticipated a phone call with updates on Linette and his baby. The moment was bittersweet, as she struggled with the absence of Kwame by her side. Unfortunately, he was not allowed to come to the hospital to see Linette give birth, due to prison regulations and restrictions. He was initially unaware of Linette being in labor because he didn't receive any phone calls. Linette was not allowed to make phone calls because it was after the allotted calling hours.

As soon as she gave birth, her baby girl was

snatched from her arms robbing her of bonding time. Linette was yelling and crying nonstop.

"Please don't take my baby! I want to hold her for a little while longer, please!"

With the jail guards watching and waiting to take her back to jail, the nurse turned and looked at Linette and said,

"I'm sorry, but I have to take the baby now."

Linette was completely heartbroken and in disbelief, wondering how this could even be lawful and legal. A baby needs its mom's nurturing.

Kwame finally got the call from the hospital nurse, instructing him on when and where he should be able to pick up his baby girl. After giving birth and a day of rest at the hospital, Linette was transferred back to the prison where she would finish the rest of her sentencing. Now, Kwame was left as a single dad, taking on the responsibility of caring for their child.

Despite the joy of becoming a mother, life remained tough for Linette. She was not only separated from her baby, but she was also trying to grasp the new changes and challenges of her post-prenatal body. Her breasts leaked milk, causing her discomfort and pain. Nights became particularly difficult as she awakened to the sensation of her milk flowing uncontrollably.

Things had gotten rough for Linette. She experienced deep depression from missing her baby girl.

Kachelle was now two months old, and Kwame filled out the form to add the baby to the visitor's list to be able to see her mom in jail. However, when Kwame brought the baby to visit her mom, the visit was denied because Kachelle's name was not yet added to the list, and the officer would not let him in with the baby. Now Linette was sad and angry. This was the first time she thought she was going to hold her baby girl, and that was all taken away from her in an instant. Linette started to have PTSD. With no real help or treatment in the jail system, she started to shut down, not coming out of her cell to eat or get fresh air.

Finally, after a month, Kachelle was added to the visiting list, and Linette got her long-awaited visit from Kwame and the baby. She had been longing for this moment to hold her baby girl. Linette woke up with so much joy. She combed her hair so she could look beautiful seeing her daughter for the first time since giving birth.

Linette got to see her baby, but it was not the joyful moment she imagined. Kachelle cried and only wanted Kwame, not Linette. This hurt her deeply. She felt lost and broken.

As time went on, Linette's emotional pain intensified, and she began questioning the value of life itself.

When she saw Kwame and Kachelle, her heart leapt, and she started crying tears of joy. She went to hold the baby, only for the baby to cry nonstop as if she could sense the sadness of the dreadful place she was in. This was severely heartbreaking to Linette because all she ever wanted was to love on her baby — to hold and nurture her baby.

Linette felt so lost because this was the moment she had been waiting for. Now that Kwame was finally able to bring Kachelle to visit, things were not what she expected because Kachelle was turning into a daddy's girl. Whenever Kwame brought Kachelle to visit Linette, the baby cried and did not want Linette to hold her; she only wanted Kwame. This really took a toll on Linette. Linette called for the guards to take her back to her cell because she was so heartbroken that her baby cried nonstop and wouldn't even allow her to touch her.

Linette was stuck in her cell in deep thought, with tears running down her face as she tried to make sense of her life. She questioned whether her life was still worth living anymore.

CHAPTER 6
DADDY'S DUTY

Kwame was awakened by Kachelle crying very loudly, so he went to her crib and picked her up. She was very warm, and he noticed her hands were swollen. He rushed her to the emergency room, and when he got there, they began to run several tests because her fever had skyrocketed to 103.5 degrees. Kwame was waiting in the visiting room while Kachelle was still in the ICU with the medical team, and he became very worried and anxious because he didn't know what was happening to his baby girl.

After waiting a couple of hours, Kwame was informed by the doctor that Kachelle had sickle cell anemia, a group of disorders that causes red blood cells to become misshapen and broken down. Now Kachelle would have to be admitted to the hospital for treatment, but unfortunately, this condition could not be cured. All the doctors could do was give her treatment through IV fluids, pain medication, and blood transfusions.

Life for Kwame as a single dad was already hard enough, but now he was struggling even more being a single dad to a sickly baby with no cure for her illness. Kachelle had to remain in the hospital under medical supervision for five more days until her vital signs became stable. When Kwame finally updated Linette about Kachelle's illness, she felt helpless and defeated. As a mother, all she wanted to do was help her baby and nurse her back to health. Linette was feeling very guilty about the actions that landed her in jail for such a long period of time and the repercussions of her actions that were keeping her away from her daughter. She was filled with so much anger about not seeing her child and not being able to nurse her baby. Her breasts were still swollen, tender, and constantly running milk.

As time went on, Kachelle was in and out of the hospital almost every other week. Kwame was really having a hard time balancing as he continued to work to provide for his family while trying to care for his sick daughter, plus making sure he squeezed in time to visit Linette in jail. Kwame's mother Cookie was there by his side to help with the baby; however,

Linette's mom, Netta, refused to come to the hospital or help Kwame with Kachelle. She even refused to visit her daughter Linette in jail. Even with all the stress going on in Linette's life, she kept studying and doing her schoolwork. Her goal was to get her GED before she got out of prison.

Kwame started to visit more as Kachelle got bigger and started crawling. She still cried during visits with her mother in jail, not really wanting Linette to hold her. Linette, juggling so many things in her head, felt lonely and started to question Kwame's love for her, wondering if he had someone on the side around their daughter. Kwame reassured her that he loved her, there was nobody else but her, and that she needed to get her life right so they could be a family when she got home.

Linette passed all her GED lessons, and the jail was having a ceremony where family members could attend the GED graduation ceremony. Kwame surprised Linette and brought Kachelle to the graduation. When Linette saw them coming in, she noticed Kachelle was walking! A tear dropped from her eyes; she was so happy to see her baby girl walking but sad at the same time because she was missing out on so much of her baby's life, even her first birthday. As time went on, Kwame continued to visit and send Linette money.

CHAPTER 7
HOME SWEET HOME

Four years passed, and Linette was released from prison on good behavior. However, she was required to be on parole at her mother Netta's house. Netta couldn't stand Kwame and the fact that he got her daughter pregnant.

On the first day of release, Linette told Kwame to come over and bring Kachelle to her mother's house; however, it took a turn for the worse because all hell broke loose once Netta laid eyes on Kwame. Netta told him neither he nor the baby were welcome to her house. Kwame thought, how could this woman be so heartless to not even care to see her own blood granddaughter, Kachelle? WOW! That hit Kwame very hard, but he didn't care because he had his own place and really didn't understand why Linette decided to take parole at her mom's house.

In order for the two to see each other, Kwame had to drive 45 minutes to pick Linette up from her mother's house and bring her to his house. Linette's mother gave her a curfew and stated if she was not going to follow her house rules, she was going to call her parole officer and send her back to jail.

Kwame and Linette both started getting tired of driving back and forth every day to see each other. Eventually, Linette put her foot down and decided to talk to her mom about wanting to be with her family and raise her baby with Kwame. She also told her mom the disrespect had to stop or else she would cut all ties with her; although, Linette's parole would still remain at her mom's house until she got settled with Kwame.

Finally, Linette and Kwame were back in each other's arms, hugging and kissing like they'd been waiting forever. Linette was feeling amazing because she hadn't been close like this to her man for four whole years. They were inseparable. They were not just holding hands–they were making out everywhere! In the shower, kitchen, living room... morning and night! Yep, they were even supper for each other. Even in the car, Linette would give Kwame some head while he was driving. He was into it but still cautious. He would murmur while moaning.

"Hey, slow down, you might make me crash!"

Things got really intense. They couldn't keep their hands off each other.

Linette and Kwame's newfound love for each other impacted their parenting and relationship with Kachelle. Having her mom around again was very unusual for her. However, Linette continued to make a real effort. She started bonding with Kachelle by doing fun mommy-daughter activities like fixing Kachelle's hair, picking cool outfits, and taking her to the park. It was a big deal because Linette missed four whole years of Kachelle's life, so this transition was not easy for Linette.

She had this big dream of buying a house for her and her family, but it was gonna take a ton of money. Here's where things got tricky—she was thinking about going back to her old ways to make that money a reality. However, she promised Kwame she wouldn't go down that road again.

CHAPTER 8
HER NEW NORMAL

Linette landed a job at UPS. A real job without dealing drugs and was doing well. Kachelle started going to preschool and things were looking up for the family—school, outings, and special nights out. But then Linette learned she was pregnant again. She felt pressured to return to what she knew best...selling drugs. This led to arguments with Kwame, who was against her going back to the streets. However, Linette was determined to buy a house and start dealing again, even while she was pregnant. She started neglecting her family, leaving Kwame to care for the kids alone. Eventually, she quit her UPS job and became a full-time drug dealer. She even got a secret apartment that Kwame didn't know about.

The tension grew thick between them. Kwame started questioning Linette about her absence and neglect, especially while she was pregnant. She reassured him that she was making money for the family, but the strain continued. Kachelle's sickle cell flare-ups worsened, and Kwame had to take her to the hospital alone while Linette was nowhere to be found. Kwame was hurt and frustrated by Linette's actions. He wondered where she was and why she was not there for the family.

Money wasn't worth the pain Linette's actions caused, and Kwame's hurt intensified. To show Linette love and support, Kwame and his mother, Cookie, planned a surprise baby shower. They were expecting another girl, so they used beautiful pink theme decorations. Kwame's family came from all around to celebrate. Linette's friends showed up, but sadly, no one from her family attended. Despite this, the baby shower was a heartwarming event. They received many lovely gifts for the baby girl. Afterward, Linette departed, leaving Kwame to carry all the gifts home alone.

While doing laundry one day, Kwame stumbled upon a rent receipt for Linette's apartment. Instead of immediately asking her about it, he decided to take a drive to the address on the receipt to figure out what was really going on. During his initial visit, he just observed, trying to understand the situation better.

Back at home, Kwame started arranging things in the baby's room and called Linette, urging her to come home so they could set up the room, stroller, and crib together. Linette briefly came home for an hour to assist. The kids were happy to see her, as she hadn't been around much.

On September 13, 2001, Linette gave birth to a baby boy named Kwame Jr. She was now forced to spend more time at home with her newborn. Kwame's mother, Netta, came over to help with the kids. Linette had been home for six weeks, and her condition was improving after the birth.

Things seemed to be going well for the family until one day, while Kwame was at the grocery store, a friend approached him. The friend expressed sympathy, saying, "I feel so bad for you because you're such a good father and boyfriend, and your girlfriend is out here doing you wrong. She's playing you and has a few other guys on the side." Kwame was hurt and stunned by this revelation but chose not to confront Linette directly.

Later, when Linette fell asleep, Kwame took the opportunity to check her phone. He discovered messages from a guy named Naz, revealing that they'd been secretly involved for the past six months.

This shocking discovery left Kwame hurt and bewildered.

Later that night, fueled by anger, Kwame shoved Linette off the bed, causing her to land hard onto the floor. Filled with rage, Kwame's voice roared in anger.

"What the hell is going on?! Are you cheating on me?" In this moment, Kwame was fuming with frustration. Linette got back onto her feet.

"I'm the one taking care of this family, so keep out of my phone and stop asking questions."

Feeling heated, Linette stormed out of the house, leaving Kwame flooded with emotions. To keep track of Linette, Kwame saved Naz's number on his phone. The following morning, after their argument, Kwame tried calling Linette while getting the kids ready for school, but she didn't answer. Worrisome thoughts flooded his mind. While Kachelle was in school, Kwame asked his mother, Cookie, to look after Kwame Jr. He also contacted his sister to swap cars so he could secretly keep an eye on Linette.

As he drove down the street, he spotted Linette entering a black Acura with tinted windows.

Although he couldn't see who was in the driver's seat, the car was parked. Acting on his impulse, Kwame grabbed a sizable rock, hurled it at the car, and opened the passenger door. Linette recognized him and the car sped away. Determined, Kwame chased after them until they came to a stop. Linette stepped out to confront Kwame, who was fired up with anger at that point. As he got a clear view of Naz, the man she was involved with, Naz hastily drove off. Linette entered Kwame's car, and the two argued throughout the ride home.

Linette tried to feed Kwame lies, explaining that she and Naz were business partners. However, Kwame remained skeptical. He dialed Naz's number, but there was no response. Astonishingly, despite Kwame catching them red-handed, Linette and Naz continued their relationship in secret.

A month later, in the middle of the night, baby Kwame's cries woke Kwame up. He got up to check on the baby and realized that Linette still hadn't returned home. Concerned, he dialed her phone repeatedly, but she didn't answer. He continued for an hour, yet still, no response. Kwame decided to wake up his mom, Cookie, so she could babysit the kids while he went out to search for Linette. As he headed to the same house as before and noticed the familiar black Acura parked outside. This time, Kwame approached the door and knocked forcefully, even giving it a few kicks, but no one answered. Frustrated, he contemplated peering in through a window or even attempting to enter through one. Kwame's banging became louder and more intense until the landlord of the apartment appeared. The landlord questioned Kwame, curious about his presence on the property. Kwame's response to the landlord was stern.

"You better evict this person because I'm coming back to take serious action."

He waited in his car for a while, hoping someone would leave the apartment, but no one did. After a few hours, he headed back home, still with no sign of Linette. She hadn't picked up her phone or returned home.

Kwame's frustration grew, and he began to question their relationship. When Linette eventually returned home, another argument ignited. Kwame demanded an explanation for the existence of another apartment. He had clearly reached his limit, having shouldered the responsibility of caring for the kids on his own while Linette continued her involvement in drug dealing. He was especially upset because she had neglected her family and was not spending time with her children. Linette maintained her stance, asserting that she was earning money to buy a house. Kwame's patience was wearing thin.

On July 4, 2002, Kwame received a call that Linette had been pulled over and arrested for driving under the influence (DUI). Unfortunately, she couldn't make bail due to her parole status. A "*do not release*" order was placed on her, preventing her from being released because of her parole violation. As a result, she spent another year and a half behind bars, separated from her kids and family.

Despite his frustration, Kwame put his emotions aside for the well-being of the children. He continued to bring them to visit Linette in jail. During one of these visits, Kwame and Linette had a serious conversation about the future of their family. Linette committed to not cheating anymore and assured him that she was committed to positive change. Remarkably, even in the confines of jail, their relationship began to mend as their trust grew stronger.

After serving a year and a half, Linette was released from jail and transitioned to a halfway house, where she resided for three months. Kwame was still able to visit her, and Linette started receiving weekend passes to stay at home.

This marked a step forward for them, as they worked towards rebuilding their family and creating a more stable and secure future.

CHAPTER 9
ANOTHER CHANCE

While in the halfway house, Linette landed another job, even though she wasn't particularly pleased with the pay. She was trying everything to get out of the halfway house and back home to her two children and her man.

One day while walking back to the program from work, Linette ran into one of her old crew members named Joe. He saw her walking and pulled up on the side of her in his car and rolled down his window.

"Hey, I heard you was home. I see they got you walking." They both laugh. Joe asked if she was ready to get back to making some real money.

"Hell yeah," she replied. "You know I'm about my money. I got a family to feed now. It's just that I'm in a halfway house right now and can't move around like I want to. You know the halfway house be a bunch of bullshit. They be on our ass about getting a job and paying rent. In this place, they don't take us out job searching. They send you on a bus line and give you a short ass time to get back. But my time here is short, so I'll hit you up when I'm ready."

They exchanged numbers. Linette shook his hand and continued to walk back to the program.

After Linette got back to the halfway house, she had to do her chores around the facility. As she was sweeping the hallway, she started to come up with a plan on how she was going to keep her job and start selling drugs on the side without getting caught and in trouble, all while keeping Kwame in the dark. She immediately began a mental strategic game plan.

After a week, Linette was released from the halfway house and went back home to her family. Kwame was very overwhelmed at this point because it seemed like Linette was just going to continue with her habitual behavior, but he loved her so much that he continued with the relationship.

Now they had two children whom Kwame was raising by himself, and with him coming from a broken home, he had his heart set on being with the mother of his children and someday getting married.

Back on mommy duty, Linette tried to bond with her new baby boy, whom she had to leave at six months old. With Linette being in and out of jail, Kwame was forced to work two jobs to take care of his family, and many times he had to miss work due to Kachelle being sick often.

Linette found herself back in the drug game once again. She started building up her customers again while still working her regular job. Money began to pour in, yet she managed to keep all of this hidden from Kwame. Linette even got another car behind his back, making a comeback from her previous lifestyle. Everything was once again gaining momentum once again.

She make sure she provided a joyful Christmas for her family after missing so many holidays due to jail time. Linette dove into shopping. The ability to buy whatever she desired made her feel empowered. However, Kwame became suspicious again. Linette was back to her old ways acting like she used to, coming home late from work with extra money. He was wondering what was going on and if she was back to her old habits.

CHAPTER 10
TOUGH CHOICES AND PROMISES

Linette had a lot of money coming in now, so she'd been skipping her regular job and not showing up.

One day, she decided to be honest with Kwame. So, she sat him down.

"Listen, I'm back to selling drugs. This 9-5 job isn't enough. We need real money. I've saved up for a house. Just let me handle it, and you focus on your job and fixing your credit. We'll live well, and you will not want for anything. Trust me, I love you and I've got a plan."

Kwame gave her an *I already knew* look. Deep down, Kwame knew this wasn't right. He really wanted Linette with him and their kids so they could finally have a sense of normalcy...as a complete family. He wanted to create a family he never had as a kid, but because he loved Linette, he agreed to her plan. Kwame told her to be careful, come back to him, and stay out of trouble.

"Don't worry," Linette reassured him. "We're in this together." They shared a kiss and made love to seal their agreement.

Kwame didn't realize what he was getting into. Linette started going out more and coming home even later. To make up for it, she handed Kwame a garbage bag filled with money for him to count and stack away. Her responsibilities as a mom started to slip away. Now that Linette was the money maker for the house, her motherly duties again started to decrease. She was hardly home, and now she was spending time in bars, drinking and gambling. One night, Isiah saw her at a bar and approached her.

"You're coming with me tonight," he whispered in her ear. Linette recognized him and warned him that she didn't want to lose her family. He insisted he just missed her and left his number in her phone, but not before whispering again into her ear, "Don't be a stranger."

Linette got up and walked out as Kwame was calling her phone. As soon as he answered, he immediately started asking where she was and what time she would be home because it was late, and the kids hadn't seen her. Linette exploded on the phone, furious that he was bothering her.

"Motherfucker! Don't start calling my phone on no bullshit! I told you what I'm out here doing. Now let me handle my business until I get home."

The call ended abruptly, leaving Kwame lost. Kachelle overheard their argument. She asked Kwame about her mom, wondering why she hadn't been around and why she hadn't picked her up from school. Kwame reassured her and hugged her, saying that her mom had been busy at work and would be back soon. They shared a loving moment.

Linette was upset about Kwame's questions and decided not to go home. Instead, she met up with Naz and spent the night with him. Kwame woke up in the middle of the night, noticing Linette wasn't home. He called her, but she didn't answer. Worried, he got out of bed. He didn't know where she was or if she was okay. All night, Linette was nowhere to be found.

The next morning, Kwame got Kachelle ready for school and kept trying to reach Linette. Her phone rang, but she still didn't pick up. After dropping Kachelle off, Kwame went out looking for Linette. Eventually, she called back.

"We need to talk," Kwame began. "You can't keep leaving me to take care of the kids alone. Kachelle keeps asking for you. You're not in jail anymore, and I shouldn't have to bring them to my mother's house every time I work, while you're out doing who knows what."

"Baby, I'm sorry," Linette responded. "I had business to handle. I can't have my phone on all the time. If I talk to you, I can't get things done."

"Where are you?"

"I'll come pick you and Kwame Jr. up for lunch and shopping."

They spent time together, and Kwame was happy to have quality time with Linette. They picked up Kachelle from school, and Kachelle saw her mom and got excited.

They hugged, and Linette said, "I miss you, baby girl." They spent the rest of the day together, skating and having dinner. Linette's phone rang at dinner, and she joked,

"Time to make the donuts!" Kwame reminded her it was family night, and they were all going home together. Naz's calls kept coming, but Linette chose not to pick up. Kwame noticed the repeated calls, but he didn't say anything.

After they got home, they took a shower together and got the kids ready for bed. Despite her phone ringing persistently, Linette continued to ignore it. In the living room, she started counting money, and Kwame joined her after his shower. Their kisses turned more passionate, and they moved to the bedroom.

"Baby," Linette began. "Just give me a couple more months, and we'll have enough money to buy our first house." They cuddled up and fell asleep.

Later that night, Kwame woke up and realized Linette wasn't in bed. He called her immediately.

"Hey babe, what's up?" she answered nonchalantly. Kwame could not maintain his anger.

"Where are you? You were supposed to take Kachelle to school."

Linette was vexed.

"Look, I missed out on a lot of money yesterday and last night, but I spent time with my family. Now I have to get back to work. You know how it is." Kwame wasn't pleased and reminded her.

"Well, make sure you don't forget to pick your daughter up from school today because I have work to do."

After talking to Kwame, Linette called Naz back. He answered and immediately started yelling.

"I've been calling you all night! Why haven't you been picking up?"

Linette snapped.

"Don't start acting crazy. I was with my family, but what's up? Where are you? I'll come over soon. I just need to make a few stops, and then I'll be there."

"I'm at home," he replied.

After they hung up, Linette headed to her neighborhood hangout spot. She spotted some people shooting dice on the block and joined the game. However, luck wasn't on her side, and she was losing money. She continued playing for hours to try to recover her losses. She ignored the constant ringing of her phone because she was engrossed in the dice game.

Despite the numerous missed calls, Linette forgot about picking up Kachelle from school. Her mind was focused on the game. Kwame was at work, and when the school tried to contact him, he couldn't answer due to poor phone reception. They then tried calling Linette, but she was still engrossed in the dice game and didn't notice her phone. The school had Linette's grandma Bea's number. She answered, but she didn't drive and couldn't pick Kachelle up. Bea called Linette's mother, Netta, and explained the situation. Netta's response was cold.

"I don't care. Tell Linette to remove your name from the school emergency list. Why the hell are they calling you?" Frustrated, Bea hung up on Netta and tried to reach Kwame at his workplace. Kwame ended up leaving work early to pick up Kachelle.

As Kwame drove to the school, he noticed an incoming call from Netta on his phone. He answered and without delay, Netta started yelling.

"Remove my mother's number from the school's contact list. She can't even pick Kachelle up."

Kwame responded, "I understand that she doesn't drive, but we have her number on the list because she's usually at home and able to take calls, like she did today. However, if you want, I'll remove her name from the list."

Kwame's frustration grew.

"Where is Linette, and why didn't she pick Kachelle up from school like I asked her to? And why is it a problem to have Grandma Bea's number on the list?"

Arriving at the school, he retrieved his daughter and ensured that Grandma Bea's name was removed from the contact list.

Unable to return to work, Kwame decided to go to his mother's house since she was taking care of Kwame Jr. As he arrived, Cookie heard his car and greeted them at the door.

"Son, weren't you supposed to be at work?" She asked.

"I was at work until the school called," Kwame explained. "They said Kachelle was left at school without anyone to pick her up when school let out. Linette was supposed to do it, but you know how she is. She didn't answer her phone, and her mom called me in a frenzy, demanding that we remove Grandma Bea from the emergency contact list. She was yelling and making a big fuss over nothing, and it really got on my nerves."

Staying composed, Cookie gestured for Kwame to sit down and offered some words of wisdom.

"Don't let that stuff get to you, son. Just pray for her. God has a way of handling people like that.

Now come and eat. I made your favorite...collard greens, cornbread, and chopped barbecue. It's good."

"Mom, I'm not really in the mood to eat right now. This situation is just crazy," Kwame responded.

Cookie reassured him, "Don't worry, as I said, God's got your back."

About an hour later, with Kwame and the kids still at his mother's house, Linette finally returned his call. He rushed outside to prevent the kids from hearing him as he angrily answered the phone.

"Seriously? You forgot to pick up your daughter? I told you I had to work, and your mom called me talking nonsense because the school contacted Grandma Bea to pick her up when you didn't. Now she wants us to remove them from the emergency list."

Linette apologized.

"I'm so sorry. I was caught up in a dice game. But forget that now. Where are you? And guess what? I won! I won big! I just scored 20 grand off this game. I'm coming to get you guys. We're going shopping."

"Fine, I'm at my mom's place. I'll leave my car

here."

As Linette hurried to pick them up, Kwame got the kids ready. During the ride to the store, Kwame was still upset.

"Linette, my job is on the line, and you need to help more with the kids. I can't keep missing days from work. Today I had to leave work early to pick up our daughter."

Linette agreed to soothe his feelings and ease the tension. They arrived at the mall and then had dinner. While dining, Linette's phone constantly buzzed. Kwame noticed the incoming calls.

"I hope you're not planning to head out again. Let's watch a couple of movies with the kids until their bedtime. Plus, Kachelle needs her hair washed."

Linette agreed, but when they returned home, she fell asleep right away instead of helping with bedtime routines. Kwame was both frustrated by her disengagement and relieved that she was staying home. As he took care of the kids, he noticed her phone ringing incessantly. Despite the temptation to answer one of the calls, he refrained.

The next morning, Linette slept in, so Kwame

took the initiative to drop Kachelle off at school...
leaving Junior and Linette asleep at home.

On his way back home, he made a pit stop at a gas station to refuel. While looking for the gas button, he spotted an open box of condoms. When he picked it up, he also noticed a zip-lock bag containing a toothbrush, mouthwash, Vagisil wipes, and a small travel-size perfume bottle. Furious, Kwame abandoned the gas station without filling up and sped home.

Once he was back in the house, Linette was awake, playing with Kwame Jr. She questioned why he didn't wake her up, and Kwame confronted her about the condoms and the items he found in the car. Linette laughed at his mention of a *"hoe bag"* and demanded that he stop going through her things. Kwame got closer to her and stood his ground, reminding her that they left his car at his mom's house the previous day.

Linette walked away from the conversation, stating that she didn't have time for a fight and that she needed to head out. Kwame accused her of prioritizing the streets over spending time with the family. Linette briefly engaged with their baby and then left after grabbing her purse. She asked for her car key, but Kwame was unwilling to be left without a car due to her unpredictable behavior. Linette promised to return in an hour and take him to his car, emphasizing the risks she took for the family's sake. She headed out while Kwame took care of their child and contacted his mom to let her know he was coming to pick up his car.

Two hours later, Linette returned to take Kwame to his mother's house. Once there, she instructed him to retrieve a duffle bag from the trunk, sharing that it contained the money they would use to buy their first house. She suggested they start looking over the weekend. Kwame's face lit up, and he leaned in for a passionate French kiss, with his hands moving down suggestively. Linette responded with a flirtatious laugh, telling him to stop because she needed to get back to work. He agreed but asked her to come home that night because he desired her. She agreed and drove off.

CHAPTER 11
PRAYER CHANGES THINGS

While running errands, Kwame received a call from Kachelle's school informing him that she had a high fever and needed to be picked up. He immediately contacted Linette to inform her about the situation and to ask her to meet them at the hospital. Linette suggested that Cookie watch Kwame Jr. while she joined them at the hospital, mentioning that she was currently busy. Kwame collected Kachelle and took her to the hospital, where the medical staff attended to her promptly by drawing blood, providing IV fluids, as well as giving her pain medication. As hours passed, Linette still hadn't arrived.

The doctors entered the room and shared with Kwame that they would need to admit Kachelle and potentially perform a blood transfusion due to her sickle cell condition. Concerned, Kwame asked for more information, and the doctor reassured him that Kachelle was in capable hands. In cases of sickle cell disease, blood transfusion helps replace the problematic red blood cells, improving oxygen flow. Kwame expressed his reservations about the transfusion, however the doctor promised to discuss alternative options with the medical team.

As the doctor left, Kwame reached out to Linette to update her on the situation. Upon answering the call, he wasted no time and informed her about their daughter's condition. Worried, he urged her to hurry to the hospital. Linette responded, assuring him that she was on her way and would be there soon.

Kwame immediately dialed Cookie's number. His voice laced with concern as he shared the distressing news.

"Mom, we need prayers urgently! They're admitting Kachelle and discussing the possibility of her having a blood transfusion."

Cookie's voice held a strong resolve as she responded.

"Oh no, we won't let fear take over. Let's pray together, right now, for fast healing for my granddaughter." She paused to place the baby down. She continued. "Let me grab my Bible. We're going to read Isaiah 53:5. *'He was wounded for our transgressions, He was bruised for our iniquities; The chastisement of our peace was upon Him, and with His stripes Kachelle is healed. Amen!'*"

Cookie shifted the conversation, inquiring about Linette's whereabouts.

"Where's Linette? She should be here by now. Keep praying, son. Remember, God watches over us from above. I love you. Keep me updated, and don't hesitate to call."

Kwame's heart was touched by his mother's support. "I love you even more, Mom," he responded.

The call ended, and Cookie reached out to her own mother, Mary. Urgently, she shared the need for prayer, and together, they joined in a heartfelt plea for Kachelle's well-being.

After hours of waiting, Kachelle was finally being admitted to the 4th floor of the children's hospital, but Linette was nowhere to be seen. Kwame was left to manage the barrage of doctors and questions on his own, anxiously awaiting the team's decision regarding Kachelle's potential blood transfusion. Eventually, Linette arrived at the hospital, contacting Kwame from the emergency department to find out where they were. Kwame's anger boiled over as he confronted her, his frustration palpable.

"Don't come in here with questions. Your daughter is sick, and you should have been here. Was another dice game more important?"

Despite the tension, Linette brushed off the confrontation, avoiding further argument. Soon after, she fell asleep in a chair, and Kwame, despite his resentment, covered her with a blanket. During her slumber, her incessantly ringing phone became a source of annoyance. Kwame, trying to access her phone, found it locked. He attempted to guess the password, but his efforts proved futile. He abandoned the attempt, placing the phone back after multiple unsuccessful tries.

The following morning, at 6 am, the doctors arrived to discuss Kachelle's care plan. Kwame was quick to engage, rising from his seat while Linette continued to sleep. The doctors delivered the encouraging news that Kachelle's condition had improved, and she wouldn't require a blood transfusion. However, she would need to remain in the hospital for a few more days for further observation and treatment. Kwame's heart filled with gratitude as he awakened Cookie to share the positive update. She reassured him with a message of faith, reminding him to trust in God regardless of circumstances. Kwame then made sure that his youngest, Kwame Jr., had everything he needed before his mother returned to rest, ending the conversation with a heartfelt expression of love.

After Linette finally woke up, Kwame subtly took note of her phone's passcode as she unlocked it: a simple and memorable sequence, 7777. Linette and Kwame spent their time in the hospital playing cards, sharing meals, and enjoying each other's company. Kwame found comfort in the fact that Linette remained by his side, a departure from her usual habit of leaving abruptly.

Following four days of hospital care, the doctors decided that Kachelle was ready to be discharged. While Linette went to Cookie's house to pick up their son, Kwame took Kachelle home for some much-needed rest. During Linette's visit to Cookie's, she was greeted with a comforting meal and precious moments of togetherness. The bond between Linette and Cookie was rejuvenated, reminding them all of the importance of family and connection.

Linette headed back home with Kwame Jr. after visiting Cookie. Upon arriving, she saw Kachelle resting in bed and Kwame taking a nap on the couch. Gently placing the baby down, she surprised Kwame with dinner from his mom. Their playful and affectionate gestures filled the room with warmth and smiles.

"Bae, I have dinner for you from your mom."

He smiled, "Thank you for remembering me."

She pushed him and said, "I always remember my man."

He smirked and began to blush. Linette slowly walked over to him while he was on the couch and began to kiss him seductively. As the atmosphere became more intimate, Linette leaned in and started kissing Kwame. She began to kiss him on his neck and nibble on his nipples as she made her way down to his zipper. She began to give him head as his eyes rolled back in awe. Their connection deepened, and their actions became more passionate. After a while, they lay close to each other, and Kwame opened up about his desire for them to spend more quality time together as a family and his desire for Linette to step away from selling drugs.

"I love you so much." Kwame said as he looked

deeply into her eyes. "I want you to stop selling drugs, and I need you to be around more with me and the kids as a family."

"I love you too, but Kwame, we need money. I gave you the down payment for the house. Where is the money?"

"I put the money in my account."

"Well, we can go house shopping now that Kachelle is out of the hospital."

She continued kissing him.

"Well, it's time to make the donuts. I have some running around to do, but I'll be back."

With a playful wink, Linette suggested she had some errands to run and began to head out, leaving Kwame with a smile on his face.

Linette then went to her usual hang-out spot, a bar where she had become friends with the owner. The owner had tried to talk to her the last time she was there, but she had to rush to the hospital. Her phone rang, and it was Naz calling. She arranged to meet him at the bar.

When Linette entered the bar, the owner, Andre, spotted and greeted her. He offered her a drink, her favorite Guinness...on the house. She playfully remarked about him being the bartender too, and they shared a laugh. As he put his number into her phone, Naz arrived at the bar. He acknowledged Andre with a friendly gesture and joined Linette at the table.

Naz questioned Linette about where she'd been and why she hadn't reached out. She brushed off his inquiries, explaining that she had a family and a partner who was already giving her a hard time. Naz insisted on having a drink together, and they sat down to talk. Meanwhile, the owner, Andre, discreetly waited for Naz to leave so he could have some time with Linette.

As their conversation unfolded, Linette's phone kept ringing persistently. She apologized to Naz, saying she had to leave for a while to take care of some things. Naz mentioned he would be waiting for her to come over later. They both left the bar, and Linette headed to meet her supplier for a refill. The supplier gave her what she needed, and she handed him a bag with fifty-thousand dollars. Linette cautiously drove away, mindful of avoiding any unwanted police attention.

Back home, Kwame called her multiple times. She answered briefly, explaining she was occupied and would call him back later. He asked her to come home soon, and she assured him she would before hanging up. Linette then headed back to the bar, ready for whatever the night would bring.

CHAPTER 12
LINETTE SETS UP A NEW SHOP

When Linette got back to the bar, Andre saw her coming and had a Guinness and a cold glass waiting for her. She came and sat down and said,

"Oh thanks. You remembered." Andre then sat down next to her. "So, tell me about yourself."

She looked him in his eyes with a straight face.

"What do you want to know?"

"Where you from? Do you have a man?"

"Well damn, are you the police? You're being mighty nosey." She replied with a smile as they both laughed.

"I'm serious. I want to get to know you. I saw you in here earlier talking to my man Naz. I hope you ain't serious about him because all he does is creep around with everybody girl. He never got his own chick. He doesn't have any kids, but his stomach is hanging out like he had six babies."

Linette burst out laughing.

"Chill. My name is Linette, but people in the streets call me Peaches. I have a husband and five boyfriends, and once a month, we all sit and have dinner. They put their names on my calendar since I don't want any fighting."

He turned and looked at her in a state of shock. "I KNOW YOU FUCKIN LYING! Stop playing with me," he said while gently pulling her close to him.

She laughed at him.

"Get your hands off of me," Linette said coyly.

The two continued talking and drinking until the end of the night when it was time for the bar to close.

"Why don't you come with me? We can go get some food," Andre asked. Linette stopped and thought for a minute.

"Let me talk to you in private," Linette said.

Andre came over to her. "What up?"

They walked out to Linette's car, where she easily convinced him to let her start holding her drugs inside his back office. Because he wanted her so badly, he agreed without hesitation. Linette went into the trunk of her car to gather her duffle bag and brought it in with two birds she just bought prior to coming to the bar. Andre told her that everything was gonna be safe and that he was the only one with a key. He assured her that in the morning he would make her a spare key so that she would have access anytime she wanted.

Andre locked up the bar for the night. He walked and got in his car, Linette got in her car, and they both drove off. They stopped to get food at the diner. It was now 2:00 a.m., and Kwame Jr. woke up crying. Kwame noticed that Linette still was not home. After changing and rocking the baby back to sleep, he called Linette's phone back-to-back, but there was no answer. She saw his number and forwarded him right to voicemail. He tried calling a few more times, but still, she did not pick up. He lay back down.

As Linette and Andre were leaving the diner laughing and talking, Linette's phone accidentally called Kwame. He answered the phone, "Hello?" but all he could hear in the background was Linette laughing.

He quickly started yelling into the phone.

"Hello?! Hello?! Hello...Linette?!"

As he started to listen more closely, all he heard was Linette and a guy's voice laughing and joking. Linette was neither responding, nor did she realize that her phone butt-dialed Kwame. He sat there stuck, not knowing if he should hang up and call back hoping she would pick up, or if he should go out looking for her to see who she was with. He thought about driving around in the hopes of catching her out until he remembered that he had the kids, who were sleeping. Now he was fuming with anger and hurt because of all the times Linette had left him home alone with the kids. He decided to call back-to-back again, but now the calls were going straight to voicemail. Linette had turned her phone off and was spending the rest of the night with Andre.

The next morning, Kwame woke up and got the kids ready. He dropped Kachelle off at school and brought Kwame Jr. to his mother's house. When he arrived at Cookie's house, he began to break his silence and started venting to her about every little thing he had been dealing with at home. He was getting tired of Linette being in the streets, leaving only him to raise the children by himself. She had not been home, nor had she spent any time with the kids.

Frustrated, Kwame said, "Mom, I work forty hours a week, plus take care of the kids full time, with no help from her. She never answers the phone when I call. It could be an emergency with the kids, and she doesn't even have the decency to pick up to see what's going on, much less call me back. She knows damn well our daughter is sick."

"Son, just keep praying, for God is going to work things out. I'm going to give you some scriptures to read, and I want you to come to church on Sunday."

"Ok mom. I love you, but I have to go. I can't be late for work again. I've been missing enough days because of Linette." He hugged and kissed his mom and his son as he left out for work. Kwame decided that he was no longer going to call Linette because he refused to let her ruin his day at work. He just wanted to have a stress-free day and kept hoping that God would change the situation like his mom said.

The following morning when Linette woke up, she and Andre headed back to the bar so Linette could get back to work. Andre let Linette in the bar and left her there, telling her he had to run some errands. He also surprised her with a key to the bar and his office. Linette got straight to business and began cooking and bagging her work in the office. Linette started to spread the word to her customers that she would now be at the bar, and that is where they could come to see her. She came up with an operation plan for the bar. This was the perfect money move for her to push her work. During bar hours, she began to make way more money just sitting in the bar playing pool and drinking.

Kwame was off from work. He still had not heard from Linette all day. He went to pick up Kachelle from school and then picked the baby up from his mother. On the ride home, he stopped to let Grandma Bea see the kids and to see if Linette had been over there. He visited Grandma Bea for a while, and she was very happy to see him and the kids. But still no Linette.

Now it had been four days, and Kwame had not seen or heard from Linette. At this point, he was very upset and disappointed in her, but he just continued to care for his kids and managed to hold his job down.

Kwame woke up Sunday morning and decided he was going to take his mother's advice and go to church. As he was getting ready to leave the house, he noticed his phone ringing. It was Linette, but he didn't answer it. She called back again.

"What Linette?" he answered fuming.

"Don't you see me calling you? What are y'all doing?"

He responded with anger in his voice. "We're about to go to church, and you need to come with us and get out of those streets."

"I'm busy right now, but I can bring you some money to put in the church offering basket for me."

"Ok hurry up. I don't want to be late."

Linette came home, and as she walked into the house, Kwame noticed that, once again, she had a trash bag filled with money. He looked at her in disbelief.

"I know you not putting all that money in the church's offering."

"Hell no," she exclaimed. "This is for you and the kids. Count it and put it in your bank account. This is why I have been away. Hustling and busting my ass so we can survive."

Kwame, still upset, took the money with no further questions. Linette got in the shower while Kwame was getting the baby ready. Linette's phone started ringing. Kwame grabbed her phone and answered it.

"Hello!" But the caller quickly hung up on him. He called the number back but no answer. Kwame then started looking through her text messages and noticed numerous guys' numbers as well as sexual conversations through text messages. He tried to screenshot her messages, but he heard her getting out of the shower. He quickly put the phone down.

As Linette got out of the shower, she casually walked into the room where Kwame was at.

"Turn the cartoons on in the living room for the kids then come back and let me talk to you," she uttered seductively as she was playing inside her lovebox. He could hear how wet her pussy was and it was turning him on. Quickly, he did as he was told. Despite how upset he was, she looked too damn good to resist. He walked over and picked her up. He tossed her on the bed, and they began to make love, better yet, makeup sex. After they finished, Kwame quickly got dressed and took the kids to church.

On his way to church, he began to think about all the things he witnessed in Linette's phone. Linette had been dealing with Andre, the bar owner, for a good four months now. Not to mention she had been staying at his house and running a major drug operation from out of his bar.

One day, Kwame asked his mother to watch the kids while he hung out for a little. His plan was to try to sneak up on Linette at this bar he had been hearing her talk about. First, he drove by the bar to see if he saw her Mercedes parked outside. At first, he didn't see her car, until he took another spin around the block, only to notice her car parked on the side of the building. After finding a parking spot headed to the bar.

As he entered the bar, the music was blasting, and the bar was crowded, but no Linette. He continued walking towards the back of the bar where he finally spotted Linette. However, she was by herself playing pool. As he continued scoping the room, he saw a man come up close behind Linette, caressing her hips as she was shooting pool. In a rage, he stormed over to where she was and started yelling.

"What the fuck is going on? Who is this nigga, Linette?!" He rushed up to Andre and commenced punching him in the face. Andre stumbled to the ground with blood dripping out of his nose as he tried to fight back, but his nose was broken. Two of Andre's boys heard the commotion, and they ran over and tried to jump in the fight to help Andre.

When Kwame realized he was being jumped, he managed to reach for his pocketknife slashing Andre in the face and the back of his neck sending blood everywhere. Linette was yelling for them to stop. Kwame got up and left the bar with blood all over him. She ran behind him screaming, "Are you ok?" She thought he was the one that was cut.

"I'm not cut. I'm good. Is this the bullshit you're on Linette? After I been holding you down all these years while you're in and out of jail. I'm taking care of our kids by myself plus working a full-time job. All while you out here cheating on me with some clown ass niggas," Kwame was incensed.

While the two were standing outside, Linette heard police sirens. She told Kwame to go home and get cleaned up.

"I need to move some stuff before the cops come," she said before rushing back into the bar. Kwame left and headed to his house. When the cops pulled up to the bar, they noticed that blood was everywhere. They began to ask Linette questions, but she refused to comply with the cops, so they handcuffed her and began to search her and her car. While Linette was in the back of the cop car, she was able to get to her phone and call Kwame to tell him not to go home because the cops were on the way to arrest him. They took her to jail until Kwame turned himself in. He immediately headed to his mother's house, and as soon as he got there, he began to explain to Cookie what happened at the bar. He soon took a shower to rinse all the blood off. Right away, Cookie started praying for Kwame, but he still tried to call Linette. No answer. She and one of the niggas that was helping her were now locked up at the police station because they found three dime bags of crack cocaine in her car's armrest.

Unfortunately, there was a guy who witnessed everything and stated to police that Linette was selling drugs out the bar and that she kept them in the ceiling of the bar's bathroom. Not really knowing what was going on with Linette, Kwame called his older sis to come pick him up and take him to the police station.

Kwame and Linette were both booked and arrested. Linette had a new drug charge, and Kwame had his first charge…in life. He was charged with assault. Linette made a call and got them both bonded out. They went home, and as soon as they got inside, Linette started yelling at him.

"What the fuck was that? Why did you come down to my place where I conduct my business and start drama?"

He jumped up in her face and said, "What are you talking about? I know you fucking that nigga. I walked in and seen y'all all over each other."

"You are wrong! He lets me handle my business in the bar. I don't fuck with that nigga, so you need to stop that bullshit, and now you got a case. But don't worry I'm taking care of all that, but you got to chill."

"I love you, but I'm tired of you not showing me love or our kids no love. You never have time for us." Linette simply responded, "I love you. I told you to just let me do what I do."

CHAPTER 13
WEDDING BELLS

In an attempt to move in a positive direction, Kwame started to make plans to take his relationship to the next level, thinking that maybe with marriage, Linette would settle down and leave the streets for good. They always had great chemistry, despite their struggles, so it came as no surprise when he asked her for her hand in marriage.

"Babe, what do you think about us getting married? I don't want to go another day without us all having the same last name."

She smiled and said, "Yes I'll marry you."

The next morning, they both went to the jewelry store to pick out rings and proceeded to set a date. Two weeks later, they got married in an intimate setting. Although it was a small wedding, it was the happiest day for both of them. Linette's Aunt Ray volunteered to babysit the kids while they went away on a short honeymoon in Aruba. Kwame was so happy his dreams were all starting to come together because he and Linette had been together since childhood, and they always talked about building a family and getting married. They also dreamt of having a two-parent household, something they both never had when they were growing up. Linette made a declaration to Kwame to not only be a better mom, but to also be a great wife.

Kwame and Linette were finally in a great space. For the first six months of their marriage, life couldn't be any better. They had everything they desired — each other, a complete family, and their dream house. Well, little did Kwame know, her actions would eventually show differently.

The marriage was going well for the first six months. Linette and Kwame found a beautiful four-bedroom home with two bathrooms and a full basement. They are officially first-time homeowners. Linette was finally in a great space in her life. As a surprise, she went shopping and bought furniture for the entire house. Their new home was finally furnished with a touch of luxury. Linette had great taste. That's what Kwame loved about her. She was never a basic chick. Cookie planned a house blessing to pray over their new home and their marriage. She invited family, friends, and her prayer team to come together to bless the home. In addition to blessing the home, they all brought gifts and food. Cookie proceeded to walk through the house, room by room, saying a prayer in every room. At the end, they also prayed for God's covering and protection over Linette, Kwame, and their kids.

Since the fight at the bar, Linette had not stepped foot back there or laid eyes on Andre. She was now a married woman, and she was trying her best to move differently. However, she and Kwame were still dealing with the case against Andre and everything that took place at the bar. They had a court date coming up, and Linette wanted to persuade Andre to drop the charges against Kwame. However, Andre was still bitter and wanted Kwame to go to jail for beating him up in his bar. Kwame had never been in trouble before. Not even a speeding ticket on his record. Because of the injuries he caused Andre, Kwame was now facing a high possibility of jail time, according to the judge, who advised Kwame to hire a lawyer.

Linette decided she was going to take her chances and meet up with Andre behind Kwame's back to convince him to drop the charges. She left the house and went down to the bar and talked with Andre. When Linette walked through the door, Andre, not noticing it was Linette, yelled, "Sorry we closed." He turned around and saw Linette and was lost for words.

"Andre, what's up? We need to talk."

"Where yo man at? I don't want no problems. And by the way, congratulations. I heard you got married. So that's why I haven't seen or heard from you in months?"

"Yes, and that's why I'm here and need to talk to you about dropping these charges. I can't afford for him to go to jail. My kids need their dad. You know my background. I have been in and out of jail. I need him to take care of our kids."

"And what's in it for me?" He answered back. Linette reached over and grabbed his hardened penis as she whispered into his ear, "I know you miss me."

She gave him a big kiss on his lips and then down his neck, turning him on.

"I need you to keep this between me and you. I'm gonna make things right between you and him. Can you handle that?"

He kissed her back and said, "Yes, but under one condition. I better see you tonight, and you better answer all my calls."

"Well that's more than one condition."

"Babe, you know I miss you, and I need to see you."

"Ok, and I need to get back in your office and continue running my business."

They gave each other a big hug as a sign that they both agreed. As she walked out, Linette turned and said, "I'll call you in a little while. I have some business to handle."

CHAPTER 14
THE PLOTS THICKENS

Linette wasted no time picking up where she left off with Andre to keep her business running. She started hanging out in the bar more and sleeping with Andre the minute he decided to drop the charges. Everything happened so quickly within a week of meeting with him. To keep the peace, Andre decided to drop all charges against Kwame to keep Linette happy.

Kwame's birthday was coming up, and Linette decided to surprise him with a getaway trip to Florida and bought him a new Yukon Denali XL truck. Two days before his birthday, Linette talked with Cookie and let her know that she was going to surprise her husband with a brand-new truck and that she needed to park it in her yard, so he didn't see it. She also needed her to watch the kids while they took the trip to Florida. Cookie was very happy and excited, and she agreed. Linette went to the car dealership and purchased Kwame's birthday truck. She got a nice red bow for the hood, and she hid the truck at Cookie's house as agreed.

It was August 5, Kwame's birthday. Linette and Cookie had been working so hard to keep the surprise. Kwame suspected that he was going away on vacation because he had to take time off work. They had all their bags packed and ready. Now it was time to drop the kids off at Cookie's house. When they pulled up to her house, he still had no idea about the truck. Cookie had the truck parked down the block. Linette and Kwame pulled up with the kids. She told him to bring the kids inside and that she would be right back. He looked at her.

"Come on now. We cannot miss our flight. And where are you going?"

"Chill out and bring the kids inside. I promise I will be right back," Linette stated.

"I know you very well, and we both know you are not coming back anytime soon, as usual," Kwame responded.

Linette brushed it off and rushed to get the truck. She used her spare key and drove the truck up the block to Cookie's house. She walked back inside the house.

"I told you I was coming right back. Now come outside and help me put our bags the in car."

As soon as Kwame walked out and saw the truck, Cookie, Linette, and Kachelle yelled, "*SURPRISE!*" His jaw dropped as he fought back tears. He was so surprised and could not believe she bought his favorite truck. She gave him a big kiss and handed him the key.

He got in and started the truck. He turned the music up loud and started dancing in his seat with excitement.

"Ok kids, daddy got a new car, and y'all can't get in this one." They all started laughing as Kwame suggested, "Let's take her for a spin."

Linette interjected.

"You can drive it when we get back. We have to get to the airport."

Cookie teased, "Don't worry. I'll test drive it for you until you get back."

"Mom how are you going to drive my car before me?" Kwame chuckled.

"Because I'm watching your kids." Linette high-fived her, and they both laughed. Linette and

Kwame headed to the airport.

When they arrived in Miami, Linette had a beautiful room with a Jacuzzi and Spa services. She also rented a drop-top Porsche. Kwame was so happy to be enjoying his birthday with Linette instead of visiting her in prison. They went shopping and out to eat dinner. While looking for things to do, Linette found out Musiq Soulchild was doing a concert in Miami. She bought front-row tickets to see Musiq Soulchild, since that is Kwame's favorite artist. Kwame could not believe he had front-row seats to see his favorite artist.

The next morning, Linette had a romantic picnic brunch on the beach set up for them. As the two lay on the beach, Linette posed in her sexy two-piece swimsuit and Kwame in his polo swim trunks. He began to kiss his wife and tell her how much he loved and appreciated her. He thanked her for making his birthday so special—his best celebration. She began kissing him back, and they started making out on the beach. After a few seconds of intense kissing, she lifted her head up, with spit dripping down her lips.

"Stop being nasty. People on the beach

watching us."

With the biggest grin on his face, he said, "Ain't nobody watching us. Those people are minding their own business. Now come here so I can finish unwrapping the rest of my birthday gift."

They both started laughing. As she laid on his chest, she began talking.

"I need to speak to you about something."

"What's up, talk to me baby.

"Well, I know you might be a little upset with me but I'm looking out for the best interest for our family. I went to speak with the owner of the bar and asked him to drop the charges against you."

"What?! Linette why? I didn't need you to go down there and speak for me. You still sleeping with this guy?"

She sat up. "I was never sleeping with him. You just came in there on some rah rah shit and hit the man for no reason."

"So, you going to look me in my face and say you weren't fucking that nigga."

She looked him deeply in his eyes.

"Nope I wasn't fucking that nigga, and you

know you were dead wrong. Besides, he said he was going to drop the charges against you. The next time you go back, they will be throwing the case out. And you better be good. I can't have both of us with arrest records. Who going to take care of our kids?”

“How you know he going to do it? He might change his mind.”

“He’s not going to change his mind. Plus, I need to get back to his bar and make this money. Now enough talking about that nigga. Let's finish enjoying your birthday.” Linette and Kwame stayed in Florida for an entire week.

On the next court date, all charges were dropped against Kwame. No more court for him. Andre kept his word to Linette. One night, Linette picked Kwame up, and they went out on a date night. After having dinner, Linette said, “Let’s go to the bar. I need to see a few people.”

Kwame refused. “I can’t go in that bar.”

“Yes, you can plus you’re with me. So you good.”

When they got to the bar, Andre was not there. So, Linette and Kwame started drinking and playing darts, having a good time putting money in the jukebox. After a few hours of them being in the bar, in came Andre, who noticed Linette and her husband. However, he said nothing. About twenty minutes later, Linette went up to Andre.

"When you get a minute, we need to talk to you."

He looked at her puzzledly, "Who is we?"

"I know you've seen us over there."

Andre said, "Ok, I'll be right over."

When Andre made his way over there, Linette officially introduced them to one another.

"Kwame this is Andre; he owns the bar. Andre, this is my husband Kwame, and I need y'all to make peace. Kwame, I need you to understand that I just handle my business in the bar. There's nothing going on between me and him."

Andre jumped in. "Yeah man, there's nothing going on with me and your wife. I don't want no trouble." They both shook hands, and from that day on, they started speaking and talking to each other.

Now things were really going good for Linette, and money was flowing in. Linette had connected her husband and one of her side niggas as friends. Kwame was coming out more, hanging in the bar, drinking, and watching the game. Some days, Andre served him liquor, and they both enjoyed taking shots together. Linette would be in and out of the bar handling her business. Some nights, she would go home with her husband. On other nights she would send Kwame home so that she can spend the night with Andre.

In about two weeks, little Kwame Jr. would be turning two, and Kwame told Linette he was going to plan a big birthday party for him, and he hoped her family would show up.

"I'll tell them about the party. Just plan it and tell me the cost," Linette said. So, Kwame set the date and sent out invitations.

On September 13, the morning of little Kwame Jr.'s birthday, Linette woke up and decided she wanted to go out of town shopping to buy the baby a nice outfit for the party later on. Kwame, upset about last-minute shopping.

"Why would you wait till the day of the party to find him something to wear? By the time you get back, his party is gonna be over." Kwame was vexed to say the least.

"Shut up. You always talking. I'll be back in

time," she said calmly as she got dress and left. Kwame got up and started getting the kids ready. He had to get the candy bags and make a stop for Kachelle's pain medication from the pharmacy while they waited for Linette to come back with the clothes. Kwame called and talked with his mom to make sure she was still coming to the party.

With just three hours left until the party is scheduled to started, Linette was still not back from shopping, so Kwame called her to see what time she was coming.

She picked up and said, "I'm on my way back now."

"Hurry up! You still have to pick up the cake," Kwame responded.

"I'm driving as fast as I can." They hung up.

Linette then got a call from Andre, who was just checking on her.

"I need you to do me a favor and pick my son's cake up and drop it off at Chuck E. Cheese," she asked of him.

"Sure, where is the cake, and what time do you need me to drop the cake off?" He asked.

"I'ma text you all the information," she stated.

"I hope I'm gonna see you later; you have been missing in action."

"Here we go again with this bullshit. I'll talk to you later."

Linette got home an hour before the time the party was set to start. She came right in and showed the stuff she bought for the kids. She jumped in the shower while Kwame was getting the kids dressed. Linette got dressed and told Kwame her phone had been ringing and that she had to meet a few people. She said she would meet him and the kids at the party.

Kwame wasn't really feeling her idea.

"Why can't we go together in one car? I need help bringing this stuff inside anyway."

"Just call me when you get there. I'll be right behind you." She said as she walked out.

He then hollered out, "Don't forget the cake."

Kwame pulled up Chuck E. Cheese and started calling Linette to see where she was and to get her help with the kids. After he tried calling her four times back-to-back, she didn't pick up her phone. He parked in the front and started to get the kids out of the car. When he went around to get

Kachelle from the other side, he saw Andre walking up towards the door with a big cake in his hands. Kwame was shocked to see him.

"Hey man," Andre started, "Linette asked me to pick up this cake and bring it to the party."

Kwame was perplexed. "Oh, she did?"

Andre brought the cake in and came back to help Kwame get the rest of the stuff out the car. Kwame thanked Andre and invited him to stay at the party. The party started half an hour earlier, and Linette still had not shown up. All of Kwame's sisters and family came to the party. Only Linette's cousin Marsha showed up from her side of family.

Linette finally showed up to the party just in time to sing Happy Birthday. Kwame was so hurt and embarrassed that his wife was two hours late for her own son's party; however, the party turned out great, and the kids had lots of fun. Kwame Jr. got a lot of gifts and money. At the end of the party, Kwame went over and thanked his cousin Marsha for showing up.

"You don't have to thank me. I am going to always be in my little cousin's life. I can't speak for the rest of the family, and I don't worry about them either. It's their loss," she assured him.

"I know cousin, but it just bothers me that my kids don't really know their mother's side of the family. They don't like me, and they want nothing to do with my kids. When Linette was in jail, Kachelle was in and out of the hospital. They never came to see her, not even one time, but thank God for my mom who was a huge help."

Marsha gave him a big hug. "I'm so sorry you have to deal with all this, but you keep being a good person. God is going to bless you."

After the party, Linette told Kwame to take the kids and gifts home.

"I have to go back out, and when I get home, I'll take the toys out the truck."

While everyone was helping to put the toys in the car, up walked Andre, volunteering to help drop some of the gifts off at the house. Andre followed Kwame home to help him get the kids and the gifts inside the house. After they finished, Kwame invited Andre to come back in and have a drink with him. Andre came in, and they started drinking and talking.

An hour later, Linette came home and noticed

Andre's truck parked in the yard. She walked into the house and saw them both watching the game and drinking beer.

"What y'all got going on here?" She asked.

"Nothing much. I'm about to head out. I have to close the bar up later."

"Ok I need to get something out the office before you lock up," Linette said matter of factually.

"Ok just call me."

Andre and Kwame gave each other dap. Andre left, and Kwame turned to Linette.

"What's up? Why didn't you tell me *he* was bringing cake to the party?" I know we settled our differences, but I don't know if I want him showing up at our kid's party, and now he knows where we live."

"Nigga, he came here with you," Linette fired out.

"Yes because you were too busy to help with the gifts, and not to mention, you showed up to the party two hours late."

"I 'm not about to argue with you. I'll be back. I have to get my money right."

"That's all you care about is your money. When

are me and your kids gonna come first?"

She slammed the house door and left. Kwame just looked up at the ceiling.

"God please give me strength."

CHAPTER 15
PREGNANT WITH THIRD CHILD

One morning, Linette woke up sick. She was throwing up and feeling nauseous. After a week of throwing up and not being able to keep food down, Linette got Kwame to take her to the doctor's office. When she arrived there, they ran multiple tests on her. She was negative for flu and pneumonia. However, they came back and told her she was pregnant.

"Are you sure? I haven't missed my menstrual cycle."

"Yes, you are definitely pregnant, and we can set you up with an OBGYN if you don't have one. With ultrasound, we can see how far along you are, if you decide to continue with the pregnancy," the doctors stated.

"I already have a doctor. I will call and make an appointment."

On the ride home, Kwame looked over to Linette.

"Now that you're pregnant, I want you to get out of the game and give the street life up. I can't raise another newborn by myself."

She looked at him in heaping anger.

"Who said I was keeping this baby? And don't worry, I'm not going back to jail. I'm just not sure if I want to keep this baby."

"Well, you not killing our baby," Kwame told her. Linette fell silent.

A few weeks went by, and Linette had an appointment to have an ultrasound done. She went to the appointment by herself and found out she was 13 weeks pregnant. As she was leaving her appointment, her phone rang. It was Andre. She answered it, and he started asking where she had been because he had not seen her in three days. She remained silent for a second then opened up and told him she was pregnant.

"I'm the father?" She shook her head no. He continued, "I know this baby is mine, and I have been having symptoms."

"Shut up," she teased. "And even if this baby is yours, nobody will ever know, and you better continue to keep your mouth shut."

"I know, I know. But how are you feeling? Do you need anything?"

"No, I'm fine. I'll see you later. I need to come to the bar today and make some money." They then ended the conversation.

Linette continued with the pregnancy. When she reached 31 weeks, Linette and Kwame planned this big baby shower and decided not to keep the gender of the baby a secret. On the day of the shower, Kwame's family and a few of his co-workers came. Linette's aunt Lynn flew in from San Francisco, California and some of her childhood friends came to support her as well. Kwame's cousin Tanya was the host, and she had a bunch of fun baby shower games and great prizes. While everyone was having fun playing games, in walked Andre with a bunch of huge gifts. Kwame saw Andre and went over to greet him and help him bring the gifts inside the house.

"Thank you so much. You bought all the big stuff on the registry," Kwame teased as they laughed.

The baby shower turned out beautiful. There were lots of gifts, which Andre continued to help with. Afterward, Andre told Kwame to call him if he needed any help putting the crib together.

"Thank you, man. I might take you up on that offer. I had to put together the last two cribs, and it was not easy," Kwame said with gratitude.

Linette went straight to the bar after the baby shower was over. Kwame called her to see what time she would be coming home to help organize all the gifts they received from the baby shower.

"I'm not sure yet," Linette began. "I'm just making some money before the baby comes. I will be out the house for a few weeks."

"Sure, you will, Linette, because you don't know how to sit your ass down. You can go into labor at any minute now, and you're still hanging around that bar," Kwame expressed knowing Linette was going to rebuttal.

"Let me do what I need to do," Linette shot out then hung up on him. Kwame got the kids settled and ready for bed. He stayed up, going through all the baby shower gifts and organizing the baby's room. Meanwhile, Linette went out with Andre, and she didn't get home until 3:00 a.m. When she got in, Kwame was sleeping on the couch with baby clothes all around him. She woke him up with a kiss telling him to get into bed. She promised to stay and help him finish in the morning.

One afternoon, as the weeks were coming to a close for Linette to deliver her baby, Kwame was at work and Cookie was at their house watching the kids. Kachelle was in a sickle cell pain crisis with no fever, luckily, but Kwame didn't want to bring her out of the house, so he had Cookie come over there to watch the kids. While there, Cookie noticed that Kachelle's pain meds were low, and she needed more pain medication. Cookie called Linette and told her to bring the medication, but Linette instead sent Andre to drop off the medication for her. After Andre dropped the medication off, Cookie immediately called Kwame at work infuriated.

"Who is this guy, Andre? And how do y'all know him?"

"Mom, he is the guy I had the fight with, but we settled things, and he has been cool ever since."

"Well, God is showing me that him and Linette are sleeping together, and that might be his baby. I saw all those gifts he brought to the shower."

"Mom, hold up, that's my baby, and he and Linette are not sleeping together. Go take care of my kids, and I'll see you after work," then he hung up. He looked up and started talking to God.

"Lord, give me strength." He knew deep down that whenever his mother heard from God, she was usually spot on. Kwame got back to work while trying to block out what his mother was saying about Andre and Linette.

On June 10 at 4:30 a.m., Linette awakened out of her sleep and noticed the bed was wet. She realized her water had broken, and she instantly shook Kwame awake. He called Cookie to come stay with the kids as he rushed Linette to the hospital.

After 15 hours of hard labor, Linette gave birth to the cutest high yellow, green-eyed baby boy, weighing 6 pounds and 11 ounces. Kwame and Linette were both filled with joy. Kwame stared at Linette with such admiration as he kissed her forehead, telling her she did a good job delivering their baby. She disagreed.

"I think this was the worst delivery ever. I was in so much pain, but I am just glad he is here. Now I can get my body snatched with this mommy makeover. We still have to come up with a name but not today. I need some rest. I'm exhausted."

Kwame stayed the first night with Linette and the baby at the hospital. The next morning, the nurse brought the baby into the room from the nursery. Linette then proceeded to sign the papers to provide consent for the baby to be circumcised and to receive shots. Kwame left to pick up his mother and the kids to bring them back to the hospital to see Linette and the new baby boy.

Cookie, the kids, and some of the family members came to the hospital. While everyone was in the room with Linette and the baby, another unexpected visitor arrived at the hospital. However, Linette had already reached her maximum visitations for the day. Kwame went to the front desk to inquire about this unexpected visitor and to see what was going on. When he got to the nurse's station, he saw that it was Andre, with flowers, balloons, and a card. He greeted him.

"Hey, I heard Linette had the baby. I just came to see how she and the baby were doing."

"Wow, thank you, man, but we have a room filled with family members, and there's no more room for visitors. But I'll wait out here, and you can drop in for a quick minute."

Andre got excited and walked into the room saying hello to everyone. Linette was in shock that Andre showed up at the hospital without calling or texting first. When Cookie saw Andre enter the room, she immediately rolled her eyes and refused to speak. She just sat back and paid close attention as she moved with discernment. After three days of being in the hospital, she was finally able to go home with her new baby boy, Kanye.

After six weeks, Linette was back home taking care of her new bundle of joy and her other two kids. Kwame had been working overtime at his job and coming home later than usual. One Friday night, Kwame came home, and Linette's cousin and Andre were in the house. Linette and her cousin were laughing and talking while Andre was holding baby Kanye.

Kwame walked in confused, "Hey what's going on?"

"Hi bae, how was work?" Linette responded and kissed him on the cheek.

"Work was stressful at the office today. I just want to take a hot shower and lay down."

Linette retorted, "Oh no! I want to lay down too. These kids have been driving me crazy all day, and baby Kanye is getting spoiled by the minute. All he wants is breasts and hands all day."

He looked at her and laughed. "Well, ain't that something. Now you see what I had to deal with when you weren't here." He went and took a shower. Linette's cousin noticed a shift in the room's energy.

"Well girl, I'm leaving now. Plus, I see your husband wants some family time."

Linette hugged her. "Thank you for coming to see me, and don't be a stranger."

While Andre was still sitting on the couch holding the baby, Linette looked over to him.

"Ok, Andre, please put him down and stop spoiling him."

Andre handed Linette the baby.

"Ok I'm going to head out then. I have to close the bar up later."

As he started towards the door, he tried to kiss her, but she pushed him away.

"Stop, you doing too much right now."

He whispered, "But babe I miss you." She hurried up and pushed him out the door, as she could hear Kwame coming down the steps.

Once Kwame got downstairs and noticed that everyone left, he picked up baby Kanye from the bassinet and started talking to him in his baby voice. Kachelle and Kwame Jr. both came running down the steps, excited to see their dad, but they were a little jealous of the new baby getting all the attention. While Kwame was busy playing with the kids, Linette went and took a shower but forgot her phone on the kitchen counter was charging. It began ringing. Kwame heard the phone ringing and walked over to see who was calling back-to-back; however, it was an unknown caller. He picked the phone up, but the caller hung up. The phone rang again. He picked up, but this time, they didn't hang up. They just stayed on the phone, listening to him as he kept saying hello. He hung up after no response. He went back to playing with the kids, but 15 minutes later, her phone rang again.

He rushed to answer phone, and this time, he heard a guy's voice say, "Why you keep picking up my girl's phone?"

"Who is your girl because the last time I checked; this phone belongs to my wife!?"

The guy on the other end responded.

"I know whose phone this is," and hung up.

Kwame yelled, "Fuck you!" and slammed her phone.

Linette rushed downstairs after hearing him yelling and shouting.

"Babe what's going on?" Linette rushed in.

"Just some lame thug blowing up your cell."

She rushed over and quickly snatched her phone out of his hand.

"Why are you picking up my phone? And I don't know who you are talking about." Walking away, he responded.

"Well, if you don't know who might be blowing up your phone, then we should just leave it alone then."

CHAPTER 16
TRUE COLORS

Linette went for her follow-up visit with her OB/GYN after giving birth. The doctor cleared her to go back to regular duties. After leaving the doctor's office, she stopped at the mall to do some shopping for her and the children. In the mall, she saw her mother Netta, whom she had not seen or talked to since she got out of jail.

She walked over with a faux greeting.

"Hi mother, how are you? When are you coming to see your grandchildren?"

Netta smirked. "Why don't you just drop them at my house this weekend? I just got a job at the correctional facility, and I'm having a big cookout in my backyard to celebrate."

Linette, continuing her façade, hugged her.

"Oh, congratulations *mom*. I am happy for you. Well, I'll see you this weekend then. I have to hurry up and finish shopping so I can get back to the baby. This breastfeeding is driving me crazy."

As Linette continued to shop, in walked Andre, who saw Linette, but she didn't notice him. He walked up behind her, pulling her close to him then whispered into her ear.

"You are coming home with me."
She pushed him off her. "Stop playing. You scared me."

He laughed then started walking and talking as she continued to shop. Netta saw them and came over. "Well, well…who is this?"

"Mom, this Andre, and Andre, this is my mother, Netta."

She shook his hand, "Hi, nice to meet you."

They both began a conversation with each other. By the time they all finished talking and shopping, Netta invited Andre to her cookout on Saturday. He happily accepted the verbal invitation promising he would be there.

Linette went home after shopping at the mall. When she walked in the front door, baby Kanye was yelling at the top of his little lungs. Kwame was rocking him and trying to soothe him.

Kwame was agitated. "What took you so long? He's hungry, and you didn't pump any milk."

Linette dropped all her bags at the door and ran to wash her hands, then she began taking her left breast out to feed him. As she was breastfeeding Kanye, she said to Kwame that her mom invited them over to a family cookout planned for Saturday, and she wanted to see the kids there.

"Ok you can take the kids; you know your mother don't fuck with me," Kwame uttered.

"We're all going over there as a family," Linette replied.

Saturday came, and everyone was getting ready for Netta's big cookout. Linette was home getting the kids ready, but Kwame was still in bed. He was dreading being around Linette's family. Nevertheless, they all still showed up at Netta's house for the cookout. In addition to the family and friends, Andre showed up to the party with some liquor. When he got there, Netta welcomed him with open arms and introduced him to friends and family. She told him to make himself comfortable and at home.

Two hours later, Linette, Kwame, and the kids pulled up into the driveway of Netta's house. They all got out of the car and started heading to the backyard, but as soon as Netta saw Kwame coming in with Linette, she started yelling.

"I know you didn't bring this motherfucker to my house. You know he is not welcome here!" She then stood in the middle of the backyard to make an announcement.

"May I have your attention, please? If anybody wants to see Linette and her kids, y'all have to go out to the street and see them."

Linette was in shock as she ran up to her mother.

"Why are you doing this? He is my husband! But don't worry, we are leaving." Kwame was so hurt, angry, and embarrassed. He grabbed the kids and put them back in the car. Some of Linette's cousins and Andre came out to greet them.

"Linette let's go right now!" Kwame roared out. Linette and the kids got in the car, and they pulled off. Kwame was so upset and started questioning Linette.

"What is Andre doing at your mother's house?" Kwame questioned.

"He came in the mall the other day when I was talking to my mom, and I introduced them, and she told him about the cookout. I didn't think he really was gonna show up or that she'd even let him in."

Kwame replied, "Wow, she can let a nigga she just met into her house, but I am your husband, the father to her grandkids, who she doesn't make time to come see at all? I am her son-in-law, and I'm not even welcome in her house. This some bull, Linette."

Linette remained quiet the entire ride home. Once they got home, Linette helped bring the children into the house, and she started pumping her breasts to make bottles for baby Kanye.

"Bae, I am going to try putting the baby on some baby formula because this breastfeeding is killing me."

He looked at her, still upset.

"I don't care what you do. I am tired of all this disrespectful shit from you and your family." Kwame got his shoes and started walking towards the door.

"Where are you going?" He just walked out and slammed the door behind him.

Kwame jumped in his truck, turned his music up loud, and pulled off at fast speed. He got on the highway and drove 30 minutes into another town. He found a Jamaican social club and decided to check it out. When he walked into the club, he noticed people drinking and playing dominoes. Kwame took a seat at the bar and decided to watch the game. A curvy Afro-Latina woman named Barbara noticed him from across the room and walked up to him to introduce herself.

"Can you play dominoes?"

He smiled. "Yes. I learned how to play as a kid in Jamaica."

"Well come, let's me and you start a game."

They began to play as Barbara called for the bartender to bring over two rum punches. Kwame was now on his fifth rum punch and still playing dominoes.

Linette started calling him because it was now 12 midnight, and he was not home yet. She had not heard from him since he left the house upset. He noticed Linette's number calling back-to-back, but he continued to decline the calls.

As the bar was near closing hours, Barbara flirtatiously asked for his number. They both exchanged phone numbers.

Kwame was now over his drinking limit, and

he was feeling good. He headed home but Linette and the kids were all sleeping. Linette heard him getting in the shower as she got up and walked in on him.

"Where have you been? I 've been calling you. because I needed to handle some business, but I had the kids all day." He shook his head and continued to shower, refusing to talk to Linette.

"Oh, so you not speaking to me now?" Linette turned to go back to bed. When he got out of the shower, he headed straight to the kitchen to make himself a ham sandwich. While eating, he randomly got a good night text with a kissing emoji from Barbara. He blushed but refused to respond. As much as he liked the attention, he didn't feed into his lustful desire for Barbara. He took a deep breath and went into his man cave to watch TV.

The next morning Linette woke up frustrated and decided to hit the streets to handle unfinished business, all while leaving Kwame and the kids sleeping. While making her runs, Linette went clothes shopping for her husband and kids.

At some point, Linette noticed that she was being followed by an unmarked car. She quickly drove home, thinking that if she could rush into the house, she could use her family as an alibi. She was now paranoid.

Linette went home and surprised her family with a bunch of clothes and some toys for the kids.

She got her husband a designer belt and designer shoes. Kwame gave her a big hug and kiss and told her how much he loved her. She told him she loved him right back.

The next day when Kwame got to work, his boss was waiting for him in his office.

"Kwame, the office received some mail that was for you, but the envelope was addressed to the office. So, I opened the letter and began to read it, and I noticed that it was for you."

He handed him the letter. Kwame said thank you and waited for his boss to walk out before he opened the letter.

Kwame sat in his chair and began to read the letter.

"Dear Kwame, I'm writing you this letter to let you know that your wife is still cheating on you. She is sleeping with Andre and having him in your home while you're at work, and I'm sorry to be the one to tell you but your last child is not yours. He is Andre's

son. I would get a blood test if I were you."

Kwame was steaming inside from what he just read. He immediately picked up the phone and called Linette to tell her about the letter.

"I don't know what you're talking about. You need to stop listening to other people."

"I'm so embarrassed they mailed this letter to my job, and my boss read the letter before me. I don't know what you got going on in these streets, but now I'm getting tired of it. They have the nerve to tell me Kanye is not my son." Kwame was livid then continued.

"Look, I'm busy. I'll see you when you get off work." She hung up on him. After a long hard day at work, Kwame was heading home, but he couldn't stop thinking about the letter that came in the mail to his job.

When he finally got home, to his surprise, Linette and the children were not there. Linette left a note on the refrigerator for him to pick up the kids from his mother's house when he got home from work. He ripped the note off the fridge and tossed it in the garbage. Quickly, he jumped in the shower to calm his nerves and do some brainstorming before heading to his mom's house to pick up the kids.

CHAPTER 17
THE KNOCK ON THE DOOR

Months passed, and Kanye was about to be one year old. He was now learning how to walk. Kwame and Linette were making plans for a big birthday party for him and taking a mini trip, so Linette planned and paid for a lavish family vacation. Linette and Kwame packed the kids up, and they drove to Virginia, where they visited this huge water park called Water Country USA. The kids were super excited to get on all the water rides. They stayed in Virginia for a week before returning home.

When they arrived home, Cookie had a small gathering at her house for Kanye's first birthday. All of Kwame's sisters showed up with their kids, friends, and other family members. Cookie made a lot of food and even had the grill going, while Kwame's cousin cooked hotdogs and hamburgers. Everyone was celebrating and having a great time at Kanye's birthday party. Linette was so grateful for all the gifts for her son and hugged Cookie for putting his party together.

One early morning, two weeks later, Linette, Kwame, and the children were all sleeping in their home when they heard a big bang on the door at 5:30 a.m. Kwame jumped up buttnaked and ran downstairs to see what the noise was all about. By the time he got halfway to the door, he saw the police had entered the house with guns drawn.

They told him to put his hands in the air and get down on the ground.

"I'm naked! Let me put on some clothes," Kwame yelled out. The other officers rushed past him with their guns drawn, asking for Linette, who was also naked upstairs in the bedroom. The FBI officers read her Miranda rights and let her get dressed in the bathroom. They explained to Kwame that she was being arrested on drug crimes and she would not be coming back home anytime soon. They allowed Kwame to put his clothes on. He asked the officer not to wake up the kids because he did not want them to witness their mother being taken away in handcuffs. As Linette was walking out of the house in handcuffs, Kwame asked her if she knew what was going on.

"No, but I love you and kids. I'll call when I can."

The FBI was now involved, and things were not looking good for Linette. The officers told Kwame what courthouse she would be going to and told him the time to show up. Kwame was very upset and hurt. He couldn't believe that Linette was in jail again, leaving him with all the responsibility as a single dad of three children this time. He called Cookie and told her what just happened. She told him that she would be right over. While waiting for his mom to come, he heard Linette's phone ring. He ran to answer the phone, but the call stopped. He tried the last code he saw her use and was able to get into her phone. He called the number back, but nobody picked up. Kwame started to investigate her messages when the doorbell rang. It was Cookie. He put the phone down and got dressed so that he could go to court for Linette's 9:30 a.m. hearing.

When he got to the court, he was not sure where to go, so he went to the clerk's office, and they directed him to the right courtroom. Kwame was in the courtroom for about 30 minutes before they called Linette's case. The court appointed her an attorney. When her case was called, she did not come out to see the judge. Only her attorney stood up in front of the judge regarding her case. They took her to jail and continued the case for three more weeks.

Kwame was able to go and speak to her lawyer, who informed him that Linette was being transferred to a federal detention center. This time, she would not be able to make the cash bond because the federal court was requesting a property bond for bail. Kwame went home waiting to hear from Linette to find out exactly what was going on. Just when he thought the day couldn't get any worse, Cookie called to say Kachelle was not feeling well and that she needed to be picked up from school.

The night had come, and Kwame still hadn't heard from Linette. Out of curiosity, he lay down and started going through the messages on her phone. While reading her texts, his stomach was in knots and his heart was beating fast.

He thought to himself, "*This bitch really was out here fucking all these ugly ass bum niggas…Nate, Naz, Paul, Chris.*"

The one person he was curious about was Andre and his relationship with Linette. However, when he checked their text messages, there were only texts about her money. Kwame fell asleep.

The next morning, bright and early, his phone rang, but it was an unknown caller. As he saw this, his face lit up at the possibility of it being Linette. When he picked up, he was happy to find out that it was Linette making a prepaid collect call from jail.

"Hey baby what's up?" Kwame happily answered the phone. "How are you? What happened in court?"

"I need to get out. We have to use the house as collateral, and I need you to call my mom and your mom because I need three houses in order to get out. I will be able to beat my case out on the streets. I don't want to talk much on the phone. So come see me, and we can talk more in person." Linette's voice was full of desperation.

"Okay bet. What is the name of the jail where you're at because the caller ID says *unknown*?"

"I'm in Rhode Island. When the phone hangs up, call up here to the jail and get the visiting information, and come see me ASAP. Where are the kids? I love y'all."

"We love you too. I didn't tell the kids or anyone

else about this. And I didn't see anything in the newspaper. You know your mother not gonna pick up the phone for me."

"Call her from my phone."

"How? Your phone is locked." She then gave him the code.

"I'm going to call you tomorrow and have you call her for me. I have to go but come see me and I love you. Kiss my babies."

As soon as the phone hung up, Kwame immediately called the jail back to get the visiting information. They told him he could come tomorrow morning. Being her husband, he was automatically placed on the list and could put money right on her books in the visiting lobby. He then called Cookie to tell her he would be leaving the kids at her house because he was going to visit Linette in the morning, not to mention it was a two-hour drive. She agreed to keep the kids.

The next morning, Kwame woke up early so that he could make the visitation on time. He finally arrived to visit Linette, and they were both happy to see each other. Linette told him everything that happened in court. She also told him where all her money was hidden and what to do to help her make bond and fight her case from the outside. He decided not to say anything about all the messages he saw on her phone.

After leaving the visit, Kwame went straight to Andre's bar. As soon as he walked in, Andre saw him. "Hey man, what's up? You want a drink?"

Kwame, trying not to show his anger towards him so he put on a fake smile.

"No, I need to talk to you in the back."

Andre was in shock. "What's up? Everything okay?"

They then headed into the office.

"I'm here to pick up Linette's money."

"Well, where is Linette?" Andre was wondering what was going on.

"She is home, not feeling well, and she sent me over here to handle everything. Also, she wants you to keep running the business as you've been doing, and going forward, I'll be picking up the money every week until further notice." Kwame strongly stated.

To Andre's surprise, Kwame used the code Linette gave him and opened the safe. Kwame's eyes got so big when he saw that Linette had one million dollars in the safe. He had to leave and get a bigger duffle bag to fit all the money in it.

On his ride back home, he started to think and came up with a plan on how he was going to get his wife out of jail. He thought of opening fiduciary accounts for the kids to put this money in. This way the money would be protected in all three of the kid's accounts.

Linette called Kwame to make sure he made it back home safely from the visit and to see if he remembered all the information she had given him. The next morning, Kwame decided to drive to Netta's house because he had been calling her phone, but she was not picking up.

After he pulled up, he saw her car in the driveway, so he knew she was home. He sat in the car and said a prayer for her before getting out because he knew showing up at her door would cause major problems. But at this point, he didn't care. He loved his wife and was eager to get her out of jail, by any means necessary.

Kwame proceeded to knock on the door. No sooner than Netta opened it with a mean face, her fiery words were to be expected.

"Why the fuck are you knocking on my door?"

"Hey, Linette is in federal jail, and she needs your help to get out. She wants you to come to see her and will explain everything to you in person."

"I work for the department of corrections. I can't go visit her."

"Well, she needs you to give you some very important information about your house. So far, I am going to put up my house, my mom is going to use her house, and a good friend of hers, Harvey, will add her house as well. All we need is one more and that'll be yours."

"Well, I just mailed my mortgage payment off, so I don't have the information right now. I don't remember the name of my mortgage company. I will have to wait for them to send me a new billing statement for next month, and Linette also told me she was going to give me some money. Tell her I still need it ASAP."

"Okay, I will make sure you get the money. Also, let me know when you get the details for the house. Her lawyer is waiting so he can get her a bond hearing in front of the judge this week."

Netta agreed.

Kwame left and went to the bank to take out money for Netta, in hopes that she would add her house as collateral to get Linette out of jail. He called Netta, and she told him he could leave the money in her mailbox because she had a lock on it, and nobody could get in it but her. Plus, she had already left for work. He dropped the envelope in the slot of her mailbox and left.

CHAPTER 18
NO LOVE FROM MOM

Three months passed, and Netta had not picked up her phone since Kwame left the money in her mailbox. Everyone else had turned in all the information needed for Linette to make bond. She was just waiting on information for her mom's house. Linette had been to court twice since her arrest.

Kwame was now forced to take a leave of absence from work. He started making drops and collecting money from Linette's business. With all the money coming in and the money Linette had stashed, Kwame took a large lump of the money and opened a safety deposit box. Before long, Kwame found himself taking over his wife's drug business entirely.

Linette decided to take her case to trial after talking with her lawyer about all the information that the state's attorney had against her. When Kwame went to visit Linette, she explained to him her reasons for taking her case to trial. Kwame expressed some concerns about what would happen if she lost her case at trial.

Linette kissed him. "Don't worry, everything is gonna be alright, and I'll be back home soon. They can't hold me forever. I just need you to keep stacking the money up.

"Ok, I'll do that. Oh, by the way, have you talked to your mother? She still hasn't called me back.

"Fuck her! I can't worry about that now. I have to stay focused and beat this case."

"Well, I hate to be the one to tell you, but your mother is a fraud. She's claiming that she can't come see you or accept any of your calls because she works for the department of corrections. My sis Kathy went to the prison two weeks ago to visit her friend, and she said your mother was in the front building answering phones." He laughed.

"She didn't even have a uniform on. She was in regular clothes. She is just a fucking secretary. All she does is answer phones. She doesn't even sign in the visitors. She acting like she's the warden or some shit. Plus, you have a federal case, not a state case.

That's so fucked up. She don't even want to help her own daughter."

Linette replied, "It is what it is.

CHAPTER 19
SLEEPING WITH A RAT

A few months passed and Linette's trial began. Kwame, his mother, and Linette's Aunt Lynn flew in for support. Linette's lawyer called Kwame and explained how things would go in court and that he needed to bring some dress clothes for Linette to wear in court. The court date was set for jury selection, where the court picked the twelve jurors. After three days of picking jurors, the trial was set to start a week later.

A week after the trial started, all the evidence from her motion of discovery along with voice recordings were played in the courtroom. Right away, Linette knew who had ratted her out and stabbed her in the back. It was a guy named Sheldon who worked at the bank. They met while living at the halfway house together. Sheldon was a huge asset for Linette because he opened bank accounts for her to hide her money and keep it safe. He also played a huge role in helping with money laundering, as he would help her get credit cards in other customers' names.

The FBI agents had been watching Sheldon for some time now because his bank was constantly getting robbed. He was the inside source behind all these robberies, so the FBI had been watching Sheldon and tracing all his steps with his money laundering for a while before he even met Linette. That's when the FBI caught on to Sheldon and Linette's scheme, and that's when the FBI caught on to Linette operating in the drug business. This was yet another revelation that Linette was being sneaky all along behind her husband's back.

Kwame was hurt and taken aback by all this new information he was learning about his wife. He was in complete shock. Linette couldn't even look Kwame in the eye. She held her head down in shame as Kwame stared at her, with tears welling up in his eyes, filled with betrayal and disappointment.

Shortly after, Sheldon was called to the stand to testify against Linette to save himself. Just when Kwame thought it couldn't get any worse, he quickly learned about Sheldon and Linette's love affair in addition to their side hustle together. During Sheldon's testimony, he shared his love for Linette and was hurt that she led him on and didn't end up leaving her husband for him as promised. He felt used and taken advantage of.

Once Sheldon stepped down from the stand and left the courtroom to go outside for some fresh air, Kwame, filled with a rush of emotions, ran after him, burst through the courtroom doors, and charged at him. The US Marshals quickly grabbed him as he broke down in rage.

"You thought you could take my wife from me and break up my family? You piece of shit! You may have had the fruit, but it was forbidden fruit." As Sheldon continued to walk away, he chuckled while shaking his head.

The US Marshals released Kwame but not before giving him a stern warning. He returned to the courtroom. The court was adjourned, and he saw Linette being escorted to the holding area until she was returned to prison. Kwame felt as if someone ripped his heart out of his chest. He walked out of the courtroom, lost for words.

For the remainder of the day, Kwame waited by the phone, hoping to get a call from Linette to explain what took place in court. He waited for some form of apology, but nothing from Linette.

The next day, Kwame paid Linette an unexpected visit to gain some clarity. When Linette saw Kwame, she still refused to come clean, and she denied ever being with Sheldon. All Kwame wanted was for her to come clean and at least pay him that little bit of respect.

"I am out here raising and protecting our family. I am riding for you, and this is the thanks I get. You out here doing stupid shit behind my back." Linette was still lost for words and denied the allegations.

Kwame finally revealed to Linette that he wanted to get a DNA test for their children because he didn't know who or what to believe anymore. As he stood up to walk away, she yelled out.

"Okay I'm sorry. I'll come clean. Just please don't leave me and take my family away from me." Kwame, against his better judgement, decided to sit back down and hear what Linette had to say, as he braced himself.

Linette revealed to Kwame that she had been unfaithful. She did have an affair with Sheldon and Andre. She also revealed that there was a possibility that baby Kanye could be Andre's child.

"You had this man in our home, around our kids, and this whole time you were fucking this nigga?!" Kwame retorted.

Linette burst out crying, pleading her case and apologizing.

"I don't care what anyone thinks or says, Kanye is my son. He will always be my son. Linette, I am done with you, and you will be signing some divorce papers shortly. Now that you're in jail, I want to see these niggas come to your rescue. Cry on their shoulders because your tears mean nothing to me anymore." Kwame said as he walked away from her. He was an emotional wreck.

As Kwame reached his car, he broke down crying. Once he got inside, he began repeatedly banging on his steering wheel in heartbreak and disappointment.

CHAPTER 20
KARMA

Two months later, Linette was served with divorce papers from Kwame. Since he last laid eyes on her in prison, he had not answered any of her calls or opened any of her letters.

Kwame was granted full custody of the children since Linette was now a felon. Also, she was found guilty on all charges and sentenced to ten years behind bars for drug and money laundering.

Kwame discontinued doing business with Andre and threatened to shut his business down and expose him to the community about the drug operation tied to his bar. To make peace and to keep Kwame quiet, Andre shut down all of Linette's business and agreed to give Kwame all the remaining money he had left from it. He also confronted Andre about baby Kanye.

"I know about the affair between you and Linette. You better stay away from me and my family. I am done with you and her. And as a matter of fact, you can now have Linette all to yourself."

Kwame collected all of Linette's money. He then packed up and relocated to Texas with his kids and his mother in tow. While in Texas, Kwame found new love and quickly got married after dating his girlfriend, Michelle, for six months.

About a year later, she gave birth to two twin boys, Tyreek and Jamal. Kwame was the happiest he'd ever been. Although moving on from Linette, his first love, was very difficult and heart-wrenching, Michelle was the best thing to ever happen to him. She exposed him to a love he never knew existed.

Meanwhile, Linette had not heard from Kwame and the kids since he last visited her in prison. She was able to get a friend of hers on the outside to track him down and spy on him, only to find out he had a new woman with whom he formed a new family. She found out about Kwame's new life and relocation with their kids.

From the pictures her friend brought back to her during visitations, Linette could clearly see that Kwame and his new wife Michelle were both happy together. It was the breath of fresh air and the new beginning he'd been longing for. Linette even received pictures that were taken of Michelle playing with her kids, which was the hardest pill to swallow.

She was suffering behind bars for all her wrongdoings. Karma was by far definitely an understatement. Linette's life would never be the same again. In the blink of an eye, she lost everything — her marriage, her children, her home, her family, and all the money that she sacrificed everything for. She had lost everything over her love for the streets and of money.

Greed is such a powerful thing and easily underestimated. Her vicious pursuit of wealth and association with the streets had cost her everything she held dear to her. It was a powerful lesson in the destruction of what greed can cause.

EPILOGUE
MY TRUTH - MY SPIN

My name is Malika Carter, and I want to express my gratitude to you for joining me in exploring the depths of *The Spin*. Through this narrative, I aimed to shed light on my own experiences, filtering them through the lens of a male perspective. I was Kwame, immersed in a tale of sacrifice, turmoil, and growth.

For years, I poured my heart and soul into being the ideal wife, committed to a man who ultimately proved unworthy of my love and devotion. He was consumed by the lifestyle of the streets, prioritizing it over his family and our commitment to each other. As you delve into this story, gentlemen, consider a role reversal where all the wrongdoings you've inflicted on your partner are turned back on you. How would you handle it?

My journey was defined by a two-decade-long relationship, that was marked by an unwavering determination to salvage what I held dear. I faced the challenge of holding down a family through all the wrong choices and consequences my children and I had to endure. I stood by his side during his frequent encounters with the law, sacrificing my own peace and stability due to my commitment to my family. As a single mother, I single-handedly raised our five children, embracing the responsibilities that came my way.

Life doesn't always go as planned. My story isn't just about sacrifice; it also shows how strong we can be when faced with challenges. Sometimes, no matter how hard we try, tough situations can push us to our limits.

As you read *The Spin*, come with me on a journey to explore the themes of love, sacrifice, and unexpected challenges that shape our lives. Thank you for joining me as we unravel the complex threads of human emotions and relationships. Discovering the essence of true love and self-love has been a revelation for me, and I'm reclaiming my strength and embracing my authenticity.

Ladies, ask yourselves if the roles were reversed and you treated your partner how they treated you, would they still forgive, stay in the relationship, and remain loyal? Oftentimes, we as women sacrifice so much for others and put ourselves on the back burner. That stops NOW. Overall, fellas and ladies, know your worth. I had to learn the hard way to stop entertaining unhealed men. Hurt people hurt people is an understatement. I now understand that people can't give what they don't have. It's impossible to pour from an empty cup, especially if a man does not have love for his own mother; how in the world can he have true love for you?

For years, I held on to so much resentment because I felt betrayed and was so angry at my ex-husband for all the hurt, pain, and trauma he put me and our children through. I was sick and tired of being sick and tired for putting up with a man who neither loved me nor respected our marriage and family. I had to heal from all the hurt and pain from the cheating, the betrayal, and the embarrassment. I was constantly getting exposed to countless women. I felt like my life was a circus.

What hurt me the most was raising our children, who experienced health issues, by myself. Our son has golden heart syndrome, which caused him to be born with no ears, and he cannot hear anything without bone-anchored hearing aids

(BAHA). Our daughter has sickle-cell disease. Our son lived two years in the hospital and couldn't come home because he was such a high-risk baby. He saw every doctor under the sun. Our son is a warrior. So far, he has had 28 surgeries, including heart surgery, eye surgery, stomach surgery, and an operation on his cleft palate. Being a struggling, single black mother is already challenging to begin with. Nothing can prepare you for raising children with health issues. It was hard to hold down stable jobs because if the children had an outbreak or episode, as a mom, I had to drop everything I was doing to come to my children's rescue.

I stayed in my marriage because I didn't want my children to have a stepmom. Growing up, I was scarred because my stepmom was so cruel to me and my brother. I still don't understand why this lady hated me so much.

To this day, I still don't have a relationship with my dad anymore because he chose his wife over me and my brother. In the moments I thought my dad would step up for me and protect me, he did nothing. The last thing I wanted was for my children to experience what I went through with an evil stepmother. So, men, please be careful who you bring around your children because your children should always be your first priority. Staying with someone who doesn't have a healthy relationship with your kid(s) is detrimental to them. You are setting a bad example and scarring them for life. I am a living witness!

One thing I have also learned is you can't repay evil with evil. In hopes of getting even with my husband, I thought stepping out and cheating would make me feel better. I wanted him to hurt the same way I was hurt. In reality, I really loved my husband, and the last thing I wanted to do was to hurt him or cause my family any pain. Cheating was one of the worst decisions in my life. It was a band-aid that temporarily covered up my deeply wounded pain. It is so dangerous when we operate out of emotions. It is always a recipe for disaster. The one way to fight against people's evilness, betrayals, and all the hurt they have caused you is to dismiss them from your life. Cut off all access and turn to our Creator for healing and forgiveness.

This relationship almost cost me my life and everything I have worked so hard for. I could have gone to jail when I found out he had a baby behind my back with one of the girls he cheated on me with.

I have learned that women can be so vindictive. There are so many bitter and unhealed women out here whose purpose is to break up families and homes with their promiscuous demonic spirits. I had to take my power back by any means necessary.

I had to do the work on myself to heal as a mother to be a better person not only for me but also for the sake of my children. They don't deserve to pay for our selfish mistakes. I had to own my mess and take accountability for my actions and choices. I chose to stay in this unhealthy relationship while sacrificing my happiness and peace of mind for decades of my life that I can't get back.

Also, not having a father or father figure and experiencing a father's love left me searching for love in all the wrong places. The hardest thing I ever had to do in my entire life was to forgive my husband and my father. I had to forgive my dad, who was supposed to be the first man I ever loved. He was the reason I was brought into this world. I had to forgive him for abandoning me when I needed him the most and for betraying me by choosing his wife at the time over me and my brother. Not having that fatherly love caused me to fall in love with the wrong man and to stay in an unhealthy marriage for many years because I didn't know what true agape love in truth meant.

Forgiving my husband was so difficult because he not only hurt me, but he inflicted so much hurt and pain on our children, who are still scarred from all his behaviors. My children were even more hurt because his mom chose to not have a relationship with them, so they are not close to their father's side of the family. It's always been me and my kids against the world.

I had to forgive in order to heal, to take my power back, and to free myself. I thought holding on to the hurt and remaining angry with resentment was making my father and ex-husband suffer for what they put me through, but honestly, I was suffering. The more I stayed angry at the people who offended and hurt me, the more I was losing myself and my power.

I refuse to waste the remaining years of my life on being powerless and not living a purposeful life with joy and peace. I, Malika, choose me now and forever. I refuse to hold myself captive and sacrifice my happiness and growth for the sake of others.

I am now in the best stage of my life. I now know what true freedom, joy, peace, and happiness look and feel like. I will never allow anything or anyone to dim my light, no matter how dark life gets. God is my ultimate source and my everything. I am so grateful for my mother's unwavering love, support, and her countless prayers. There were days I felt like giving up on life, and my mom was right there by my side to help me pick up the broken pieces and keep going, with the help of God's grace and mercy. I can't find enough words to thank her for being my earth angel.

I pray that as you read this book, you will be reminded of your worth and know that you should not stay in unhealthy relationships that don't serve you or propel you forward. If anything, or anyone costs you your peace of mind and happiness, you need to serve them an eviction notice to move out of your life. Remember, what goes around comes around, and they will reap their karma. Stay strong and keep pushing forward and upward.

With Love,
Malika Carter

ABOUT THE AUTHOR

Althea Fisher, also known as Malika Carter, is from Danbury, Connecticut. She has loved film, hosting, and music since she was young. She later moved to Waterbury, where she grew up as the only girl with five brothers. Malika is also a proud mom of five.

In 2017, she made her first on-screen appearance in the series "That's A Fendy." Around that time, she began using the name Malika Carter. She became the "first lady" on ShotCallers the Show, where she shared her voice and personality. She also bartended at a local bar and hosted many private parties, building a loyal community. Her magnetic personality and love for hosting created memorable experiences for her patrons.

Malika's journey in the entertainment industry expanded even further with her second acting role in the series "City Limits." Her dedication and passion for the craft drove her to explore new horizons and continue to evolve as an artist.

Malika is now a published author with her debut book, The Spin. Her newest film project, ***Desperate Whispers***, will premiere on **November 14, 2025** in Waterbury, Connecticut.

Althea Fisher, or Malika Carter, is not just an artist and entertainer; she is a testament to the resilience of the human spirit. Her determination to follow her passions and overcome challenges demonstrates that, in life, the most inspiring stories are often written through unwavering dedication and authenticity.

Through every chapter of her life, Malika's story shows determination, creativity, and heart. She keeps pushing forward and inspiring others to do the same.

DESPERATE
WHISPERS

ACKNOWLEDGEMENTS

First, thank you God for holding me steady when life would not stop spinning. You gave me breath when I felt empty and strength when pain tried to speak louder than purpose. Every page in this book is a testimony of Your grace and mercy on my life.

To my mother, Betsy Mayo-Wingate: thank you for always showing up. Your love, your prayers, your steady praying hands. These are the rails that kept me on track when the curves came fast. You believed in me before I had words for the dream, and you stood beside me when the road got rough. I am here because you refused to let go.

To my children: I love you with everything in me. Thank you for your patience through my ups and downs, for forgiving my imperfect moments, and for trusting that, even when I didn't get it all right, I was always trying to make the best decisions for us. You are my why, my compass, my soft place to land.

To my ex-husband — thank you for your part in this story and for the ways you have shown up for our children. Our family bond is complicated but your presence has truly mattered in our lives.

To my grandmother, Reverend Mavis Bingham: though you are not here in the flesh, your prayers, wisdom, and example live in me. I hear your voice in my courage. I feel your faith in my footsteps. Thank you for lighting the path.

To Beatrice Bertha Fisher — our beloved "Grandma B" — thank you for the love and support you poured into me from my husband's side of the family. Your kindness stretched wide and welcomed me home. We carry your memory with honor.

To my family — near and far, past and present — thank you for being my backbone. Your calls, your check-ins, your laughter at just the right time, your quiet understanding when I needed space — each act of love helped me finish this work. I am made of your yeses.

To everyone who rooted for me, offered a shoulder, watched the kids, sent a text, or whispered a prayer: please know it mattered. You helped me keep going on days I wanted to quit. If your name isn't written here, it is written on my heart.

And to you, the reader: thank you for trusting me with your time and your spirit. If life has you in a spin, may these pages remind you that balance returns, joy is possible, and purpose is patient. Keep breathing. Keep believing. You are not alone.

If I missed anyone, charge it to my head and not my heart. I am deeply grateful — for every hand that held me, every voice that lifted me, and every lesson that shaped me. This book is our collective testimony.

Rev. Mavis L Bingham

Questions for Book Clubs

I. How has the main character's journey in "*The Spin*" influenced your own perspectives on love and sacrifice in your life?

II. Reflect on your understanding of family dynamics and relationships. How does the story challenge or align with your personal experiences?

III. Were there moments in the book that mirrored your own emotions or situations? How did these connections impact your reading experience?

IV. Explore how the author's storytelling and character development resonated with your own life experiences. Which characters felt most relatable, and why?

V. Did the book alter your views on the consequences of choices made for the sake of family or personal desires? How might these reflections apply to your life?

VI. Consider the role of setting in the story. How do external environments influence your own decisions and actions in various aspects of life?

VII. Delve into the theme of self-love portrayed in the book. How have you grappled with this concept personally, and how might the characters' journeys inspire your own self-love journey?

VIII. Identify pivotal scenes or events that stood out to you. How do these moments parallel or differ from significant events in your own life?

IX. Examine the impact of societal influences and external pressures on the characters. In what ways do these factors shape your own decisions and perspectives?

X. As you reflect on the book's conclusion, explore the emotions it evoked. What lingering thoughts or questions arise about the characters' futures, and how might they echo your own contemplations about the future?

Contact Author:

Malika Carter

Malika_carter_

Email: Queenfisher85@gmail.com
Nonprofit Feeding the homeless:
Mary and Mavis Project
For Donations and more information, email:
Marymavis638@gmail.com

www.ingramcontent.com/pod-product-compliance
Lightning Source LLC
Chambersburg PA
CBHW040826010826
48978CB00012BB/629